EDEN

Book 3

Georgia Le Carre

ALSO BY GEORGIA

The Billionaire Banker Series
Owned
42 Days
Besotted
Seduce Me
Love's Sacrifice

Masquerade

Pretty Wicked
(Novella)

Disfigured Love

Eden

Click on the link below to receive news of my latest releases, fabulous giveaways, and exclusive content.
http://bit.ly/10e9WdE

Cover Designer: http://www.boomingcovers.blogspot.co.uk/
Editor: http://www.loriheaford.com/
Proofreader: http:// www.nicolarheadediting.com

EDEN

Book 3

Published by Georgia Le Carre
Copyright © 2015 by Georgia Le Carre

ISBN: **978-1-910575-08-6**

You can discover more information about Georgia Le Carre
and future releases here.

https://www.facebook.com/georgia.lecarre
https://twitter.com/georgiaLeCarre
http://www.goodreads.com/GeorgiaLeCarre

ACKNOWLEDGEMENTS

Thank you so, so very much to SueBee, Caryl Milton, Elizabeth Burns, Nicola Rhead, Chelle Thompson, C.J Fallowfield, Nichole Hart, Cariad, Sandra Hayes & Lori Heaford for all your help. It is very, very much appreciated.

Contents

ONE

Jake

"Whoever fights monsters should see to it that in the process he does not become a monster. And if you gaze long enough into an abyss, the abyss will gaze back into you."
—Friedrich Nietzsche

Not many people end up sitting sprawled and dead drunk in the corridor outside their suite in a Vegas hotel. Waiting for the door to open and desperately wanting it not to. I guess I am what Edna O'Brien meant when she described the Irish character as 'maimed, stark and misshapen, but ferociously tenacious.'

In my maudlin state I contemplate a mysterious madness. If it is true that your soul alone keeps the map of your destiny, then the geography of my destiny to this expensive corridor must have been known to the highest and most hidden part of me even while I was a destitute boy. A boy who ran barefoot on grassy, sunlit meadows, visited horse fairs, and watched with hungry eyes but never touched the other traveler girls.

I have memories of digging up armfuls of carrots and potatoes, eating soda bread crusts, and dressing in rags and cast-offs even though I was the oldest. One Christmas my mother paid ten pounds for a pair of stained maroon velvet curtains in a charity shop. She cut them up and sewed all her three boys identical trousers and my sister a dress. My sister was something beautiful even then, and, of course, the dress looked gorgeous on her. I had to knock a boy down after church for staring so lustfully at her. 'Unfortunately' for me, one day after Christmas I caught my new curtain trousers on a nail and tore them so badly they were unusable even as a pair of shorts. Within a week both my brothers had 'accidentally' and irreparably ruined theirs, too.

As children we didn't know we were dirt poor because my father was a compulsive gambler. Cards, dogs, horses, sports, fights, dice. Anything that he deemed required some form of skill he found irresistible. Once he started he didn't know how to stop. Sometimes he took me with him and I used to sit big-eyed and watch him. He was my hero. What the fuck—maybe he still is.

Patrick Eden was special. While the rest of the world was telling me that the Irish were thick—'they'd bring a fork if it rained soup'—my father had a totally different philosophy.

'There are only two kinds of people in the world, my boy,' he said often and with cheerful certainty, a proud finger raised in the air, 'the Irish and those who wish they were.'

Obviously with such a philosophy he was absolutely convinced that he was a winner. The other gamblers were banking on luck, and he alone had found an infallible technique to beat the odds. And when he was winning it did seem that way. I can't forget what he was like when the pile of money in front of him was growing. Cocky? Oh! You never saw anything like my dad when he was winning. A larger than life character he was. Even now the memory brings a warm glow to my heart.

So I bought the lie. I was young and I wanted to believe. Even when the inevitable 'losing streak' struck, his confidence remained invincible. His bets became bigger, sometimes doubling. Forget doubling—every penny ended up on the table. He borrowed money from anyone who was fool enough to lend it.

This was the time desperation ruled: nothing was sacred. Everything could go into the pot. His wife. His sons. His daughter. Anything. Because he was that cocksure that a losing streak always preceded a big win. On the other side Lady Luck was waiting with open arms. He was the big winner. All he had to do was believe in himself. So he readied for the losing streak to end by betting heavily on long shots.

And then he lost.

The shock might have stopped another man in his tracks, but not my father. At that point

there was no yarn too outrageous, no lie that was beneath him. He *had to* recoup his losses. That was when he began to embezzle from the bosses. That period didn't last long.

They are bosses because they are one step ahead of everyone else.

One day he was patting me on the back, looking me in the eye and boasting about a non-existent big win on the dogs, and the next day I was being held back by two of Saul's heavies while another slit my father's throat from ear to ear. I was so shocked I went limp. I just stood and watched the blood gushing out of his severed arteries. It squirted out so far I was covered in it.

That moment can be likened to when a great tree is felled. The air becomes barren. A shocked silence ensues. The forest knows another one of its guardians has been murdered. The savagery of the waste stuns it.

My soul, dependent upon his nurture, wizened and shrank even as my mind sharpened. I watched the radiance and the light die out of his bright eyes. How they went from wide-eyed shock to nothingness. I saw with hurtful clarity all the words unsaid, the potential lost, and the promises missed. Nothing would ever be the same again. His last whisper, a gargling, unintelligible sound, was that of someone on his way to a dark, cold space.

'What do you want to do, tinker boy? Are you going to work the debt off or is your sister going to do it on her back?'

The question had only one right answer.

TWO

Jake

The next phase of my life has only one word to describe it. Saul. Before that afternoon when he made me watch his men slaughter my father like a farm animal, I had only seen him twice and spoken briefly only once. I had made a mental note: mean, dead eyes disguised by superficial charm. I was a big lad even then and I knew he always wanted me to work for him. It was only my father that had stood in the way.

What can I tell you about Saul Schitt?

Pay your fucking debts.

He hated unpaid debts. And I hated him.

I hated working for Crocodile Saul. I hated the ugly, unconscionable, inhumane things I was forced to do. And I hated the coldness that was slowly seeping into my heart. I cannot describe how it destroyed my soul to be his enforcer dog. For four fucking years I paid off my father's supposed debt on an interest rate that was calculated daily. Do you get the picture of my hatred?

I was nineteen when the debt was finally deemed paid. I went to his house.

'The debt's paid and I want out,' I said.

'You've been good to me. I want to do something for you in return,' he rasped.

When Saul wanted to do something for you, you didn't refuse. Warily, I accepted his invitation to go to Vegas with him. I had never been anywhere outside England. To me Vegas was not a destination, it was a glittering, glamorous fantasy playground that rose from the heat of the desert like a mirage. I loved it. I loved the burning heat, I loved the American accent and I fucking loved the Strip.

He checked us into the Venetian. It was amazing, I had never seen anything like it, with lofty, beautifully painted ceilings. It was my Sistine Chapel. And, shit, you should have seen the way they treated Mr. Schitt. Like he was royalty. The king of Schittland. He got the works. *Nothing* was too much trouble. They even had his favorite, a fucking key lime pie, waiting in the penthouse suite's fridge. King Schitt opened a line of credit for me. Fifty thousand dollars.

'My gift,' he said with the smiling generosity of a godfather.

In that rarefied air of unmatched opulence I became royalty too. I was so young, so naïve, it all went to my head. That Irish saying knocked on my door—what would a cat's son do but kill a mouse? I sat at the baccarat table. My father with his throat cut and blood gushing out invited, 'Have a seat, my son. There are only two kinds of people, my boy, the Irish and those who wish they were.' In a daze I sat. It turned out I was my father's son, after all.

God! How fast I lost that fifty thousand.

As if by magic Saul was by my side, smiling his benign crocodile grin. 'No problems. Extend his credit to two hundred thousand.'

I looked at my father's murderer, and you know what? At that moment, I just wanted the credit. With unutterable desperation I wanted the dirty money of that disgusting man so I could continue gambling. Like my father.

Then the strangest thing happened. I heard my mother's voice say clearly in my head, 'Even what he thinks he has shall be taken away from him.'

Luke 8: 16–18, The lesson of the lamp.

And it was like someone had flicked a switch in my head. I stood up and walked away from that table. I could feel Saul's eyes on my back, one of his men calling me back, but I was in a rage. With my father, with myself and with Saul. He had taken me and molded me into a man with vices. A man he could control.

I walked for more than an hour, without knowing where I was going, just walking in a straight line, passing dangerous, low rent areas, hardly seeing anyone, and looking for buildings in the distance.

At some point I burst open the double doors of a bar that advertised cold beers and cocktails. It was dark and seedy inside. So grimy you didn't want to touch anything. The

locals turned to look at me. Whoa! Unfriendly. This was not the Strip. Tourists unwelcome.

But I was already in and I wanted a drink. And no one was stopping me. As Saul would say, What's wrong with my fucking money? One drink and I'm out of here, I thought. I walked up to the bar and ordered me a whiskey.

The bartender, a surly guy with spiky hair, hesitated and then looked at the breadth of my shoulders and that foul light in my eyes and thought better of it. He went in search of a bottle while I looked around the bar. The exits were close enough. I let my eyes wander restlessly into the darkness. I had found out something ugly about myself.

From the shadows a woman of mixed descent got up from a chair. Ordinary looking. Black hair, brown eyes, skin like chocolate, and the kind of plump lips you know are going to be so soft when your teeth nip into them. I felt nothing. Not even curiosity about what she could be like in bed. The whiskey hit the bar surface. The measures are larger in America, but I swallowed it in one gulp, threw a note on the table, and turned to go. It was the wrong place, wrong time. The exit was ten steps away.

I must have taken five when she started singing, that ordinary brown girl. And fuck me, I froze in my tracks. I could not move.

She had the voice of a siren, you know, those mythical creatures from the Greek fables who

lured sailors to their death. As if in slow motion I turned back and looked again at her.

She was looking right at me. She was singing to me. There was nothing I could do. I was like a rat mesmerized by a cobra. From the roots of my hair to the tips of my nails I tingled with her magic. I thought—I was only nineteen, don't forget—that I was going to spontaneously combust. The chemistry was that strong. How could someone with her talent be singing in a joint like this? She should have been up there with Beyoncé and Madonna.

Afterwards, she came over to me. She almost had a smile on her face.

'Buy me drink?' she said.

The prosaic request shocked me. I had to beat down a hysterical desire to laugh. That's it? That's what you want from a man you have stunned to a slow faint?

'What do you want?' I asked.

'Champagne,' she said daringly, but her underbelly was soft.

Did a place like this even carry champagne? 'Sure,' I said.

It came then. Her first real smile. 'I knew you were good for it.'

Her name was Indigo and I felt for her. Singing in that dive, for men who wouldn't know talent if it hit them with a wet fish. I got her their best bottle, piss water as it turned out, and watched her get drunk on it. I was dizzy for her and I had a packet of condoms burning a hole in my pocket.

She lived within walking distance, so we went back to her place. The building was dark. Her apartment was at the far side. Somewhere in the gloom I could hear people talking in low voices. I gripped the Beretta in my waistband, but it didn't cross my mind to turn around and walk away. I was that wired on lust.

Her skin was smooth. She was generous. I was generous. Things got hot. Real hot. We fucked to the sound of spilling dustbins in the alley under her window. I don't know how many times. Maybe nine, maybe ten. I couldn't get enough of her. Inside her body I forgot about Saul. And his poison.

During the night it started to rain. Droplets drummed on the window.

'I haven't felt rain since I got to Vegas,' she said.

She got out of bed and went to look at the rain. You could see the drops shine silver where the streetlight illuminated them. She placed her palms and then her forehead on the cool glass. At that moment she seemed lost and sad, as if life had cheated her. Then she opened the window and allowed the rain to come into the room. She laughed as the drops hit her naked skin. She came back to me wetter and wilder. I was wrong. Life could never cheat this woman.

In the morning I lit two cigarettes and passed one to her. She was actually younger and far more beautiful without all that gunk on her face.

'I love your accent,' she said.

'Yeah?'

'Yeah. Where you from?'

'England.'

'Where Princess Diana came from?'

'Exactly.'

'So what were you doing in that bar?'

I shrugged. 'I just wandered into it by accident.'

She giggled. 'I figured you for a guy who gets on all the best guest lists and stays in one of those fancy casino hotels with white leather sofas and purple and blue lighting.'

'What makes you think that?' I was curious. She glanced at the leather trousers she had peeled off me last night. 'You've got ambition. It's in your eyes. Even in the dark, I saw it. You'll be as rich as Croesus, one day. You just wait and see.'

I felt a rush of sympathy for her. She'd never be rich or famous the way she was going. 'Listen, you have a truly beautiful voice, way better than Beyoncé. You should record a music demo and send it to some record companies.'

'Now no one after lighting a lamp covers it over with a container, or puts it under a bed; but he puts it on a lampstand, that those who come in may see the light.'

And I froze in astonishment. No fucking way. It could not be a coincidence. If I had turned left when I exited the casino. If I had gone into the bar before this one. If I had left as

soon as I saw the state of the bar. If she had not at that moment stood up to sing. I would not be lying here listening to *Luke 8: 16–18, The lesson of the lamp.*

'What are you talking about?' I croaked.

'The gates to the entertainment industry will only open for those who are willing to sell their souls in exchange for wealth and social admiration. I'm a spiritual person. I will never allow myself to be an industry puppet flashing the one-eye symbol, or making horns and pyramids and the six-six-six symbols with my hands and fingers at every photo opportunity and in every video I make. Better for my lamp to shine its light honestly in that dive you found me in last night than have it covered by the sick and the depraved.'

I looked at her and I did not see a one-night stand, a woman I had no intention of ever seeing again. She was glowing with inner beauty. I saw only the truth of the quote—All god's angels come to us disguised.

When I got back to the hotel Saul was waiting for me. His gift had morphed into a loan. I now owed him fifty thousand dollars plus interest. What did I expect? Saul Schitt hangs a black cloth over every lamp he sees.

I went back to England and for six months I laid my plans down, carefully, meticulously. I took advantage of the fact that though Saul trusted no one, other than maybe his mother, he had made the mistake of underestimating me. He thought I was a sapling clinging to his

mighty branches. He paid for his error dearly. I avenged my father's death in the gangster's way.

An eye for an eye. A life for a life.

For four years I had sat quietly in the background and absorbed the workings of Saul's little empire. No one knew it better than I. So I was confident I could take it. The sycophants never saw me coming. I behaved in the only way the power structure understood. Extreme violence. I exerted my will, established myself as top dog, and quickly took control.

But I desired a different organization.

One of the first things I did was sit down with BJ Pilkington and his father. Our families were in a generational feud, and they were not happy to be drawing up territories with me, but even they understood that I meant business. Ruthlessly I trimmed and cleaned up the organization. There would be no more dealing in class A drugs, no more human trafficking, no more prostitution, and no more loan sharking.

I reduced the rate but kept the protection racket going since abandoning it would have created a dangerous power vacuum. Besides, we would need it for the gambling dens and the clubs. I kept the contraband going too, because I'm a gypsy after all, and I have an aversion to paying taxes. Plus I'm really, really good at it.

I found myself a genius of an accountant and I started buying up properties in the most sought after areas of London through perfectly legal shell companies. And whenever possible I invested in Internet start-ups. Only two out of every twenty ventures were successful, but they were cheap to get into, they were great for washing dirty money, and when they were successful the rewards were astronomical. My best venture I sold for forty million.

Two years after that fateful trip I went back to Vegas to look for Indigo. I was the rich man she had predicted. I felt nothing for her but pure gratitude. I wanted to set her up so she could sing her songs without being a puppet of the industry. This time I didn't walk. I was driven in a limo to that bar. The sign still proclaimed cold beers, but a different barman served me.

I described her.

'Sorry, man. We've never had a singer here as far as I know. And I've been here near a year now,' he said.

Ah, Indigo. I only want to give you what you deserve: FAME, FAME, FAME.

I tried looking for her through various detective agencies, but she had left nothing but a stage name. And that was too cold a trail to follow even for the best money. In the end I had to give up. She was not meant to be found.

I thought I'd never see an angel again in my life. Until the day I came down a set of steps in my brother's club and saw Lily Hart. Here was another woman to change my life.

If she is not an angel then she is the devil in disguise.

 15

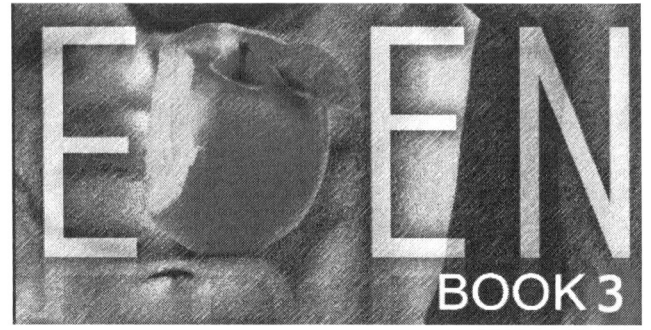

EDEN

BOOK 3

—Just gonna stand there and watch me cry
But that's alright
Because I love the way you lie
I just love the way you lie—

THREE

Lily

For a few seconds I simply stare at him in shock. It's a sight I never thought I'd see. The great Jake Eden wasted and lolling on the floor of a hotel corridor. He attempts to straighten himself by pushing his palms to the floor and fails. There is something boyish and endearing in his futile attempt. Resting on his elbows he looks up at me and wriggles an eyebrow.

'There's a whole closet of sex toys we haven't tried yet,' he says and grins seductively.

I shake my head in a disbelieving daze. 'I've booked a cab. I have to go,' I whisper.

He blinks up at me. 'I thought you wanted to see me in handcuffs.'

'I don't,' I reply tightly.

'Could have fooled me.' His voice is rolling and mellow.

I take two steps forward and crouch in front of him. His breath reeks of alcohol and his eyes are glazed. 'Well, you're wrong,' I say softly.

'No? Well, I'd like to cuff you to my bed.' His hand comes up and strokes my face clumsily. 'I don't care if you're a cop, Lily. I just want you to stay.'

The graceless, unrehearsed gesture throws me. Oh God! How much I want to stay. But I

have to leave. He is intoxicated and does not know what he is saying. I still remember the cold look in his eyes before he closed the door in the early hours of the morning and went away leaving me naked and frighteningly alone.

Confused and conflicted, I stand up. To put some distance between us I take a step back and cross my hands over my waist.

His right hand comes out to curve around my ankle. He slides his hand up my leg. 'Such soft skin. Like a baby,' he croons.

I have to make my exit, but I can't leave him in the corridor in this state. I have to get him into the room before I go.

'Can you stand?' I ask him.

'I was born standing.'

He is amusing in this state, but my cab will arrive in about thirty minutes. I reach down, take his hand and try to heave him up, but he is a dead weight. I sink down next to him.

'Come on, Jake, help me. We have to get you inside the room.'

He laughs carelessly. 'Take your panties off.'

'Stop it, Jake.'

'Just take them off and stand over me with your legs spread so I can look up your skirt into that delicious velvet darkness.'

'I'm not doing that.'

'Then I'm not going into the room,' he says, his jaw set into a stubborn line.

'I can't believe how drunk you are.'

He looks at me, his eyes not properly focused. 'Drunk is when you are over the edge. I'm not there yet. I know exactly where I am and what I am doing. Besides it is not pertinent to our discussion.'

'Well, I'm not taking my panties off and standing over you so you can look up my skirt.'

'Why not?'

'Because anyone could come along!'

He chuckles. 'That's the best bit. The fear of discovery always makes you come faster.' He slides his hands between my legs and rubs the silken crotch of my panties. His eyes glitter as his hand finds that despite my prudish objection I am already aroused by the thought. And it hasn't escaped him that I haven't swatted his hand away either. He strokes the damp material and smiles triumphantly.

'Come on, be a devil. Just one little lick. I'm dying to get my tongue inside you.' His eyes are half closed and heavy with drink and desire. I can feel myself getting more and more turned on, the material he is digging into becoming soaked.

'One little lick,' I say sternly.

'Scout's honor.'

'And then you come with me into the suite?'

'Cross my heart and hope to die,' he promises solemnly.

I stand and quickly take my panties off while he watches. Wordlessly, he holds his hand out and I put them into it. While he clumsily pockets them I furtively look right and left. The

corridor is empty so I take a step forward and stand over him with my legs spread.

He looks up and smiles broadly. 'I could die now and be happy.' He raises his eyes up to mine. 'Now squat on my face.'

I lean my palms on the wall in front of me and lower my hips until my sex is close enough to touch his mouth. Turns out it is not one little lick he wants after all. He captures my clit between his teeth so I am trapped into that horribly gauche position.

'One little lick you said,' I remind desperately.

His hands slide up my thighs and grip my bare buttocks firmly.

'I lied,' he says airily and starts sucking my clit.

'I've got a taxi coming,' I cry urgently, but the sensations that are coming from between my legs make me moan and grind myself against his teeth. I can always get another taxi. And then another voice, much stronger, says, *What happens when he sobers up? What happens when Mills and the boys at the department find out?* The thought is like a bucket of cold water in my face.

With all my strength I wrench myself away from him and stepping out of his reach stare at him panting, aroused, and terrified. 'Right, you've had your fun, now let's get you in,' I say shakily.

He holds his hand out meekly, and I take it and pull him up. He comes so easily I realize he never needed my help.

'You OK?' I ask.

'Never felt better.'

I help him to the bed. He falls on it and purposely brings me with him. With him on top of me he gazes into my eyes.

'So you are planning to leave, huh?'

'I thought you wanted me to anyway,' I whisper.

'Yeah, sure. You're one strange gal, Lily.'

'Why did you walk out then?'

He gives a bark of laughter. 'I wanted to see what you would do. I didn't realize it would take you so long to make your move.' He rolls off me and lying on his back brings out a packet of cigarettes from his shirt pocket.

I frown. 'You don't smoke?'

'I do...in times of extreme provocation.' He lights it and inhales deeply. He blows out the smoke and turns to me. 'I smoked a pack a day until I was nineteen.'

So much I don't know about him. 'What did you do when you left here?'

He makes an amused noise. 'I sat outside the room and called down and got someone to bring me a bottle and some cigarettes. They're very good here. They wanted to bring me a glass as well, but I told them not to bother.'

There is ash gathering at the end of his cigarette, and I move to find a saucer or something to use as an ashtray, but he

immediately tightens his hold on my wrist. 'Where do you think you're going, young lady? I haven't had my way with you yet.'

I put my mouth close to his ear. 'Isn't your dick a bit too limp for that?'

He laughs, a lovely deep rumble, then puts his mouth to my ear and whispers, 'I'm rock hard and hungry for you, babe.'

Suddenly my body feels tight and jittery. 'Really?'

'It's a done deal. All nine inches.'

I can't help, but smile.

'Try it and see.'

I lean back and look into his eyes. They are hazy, almost smoky with sensuality and seductive promise. I run my hand over the material of his crotch. Indeed the man is rock hard. My body instantly responds. My mouth is dry. I lick my lips. 'Let me go get an ashtray first.'

I find a glass on the coffee table and bring it back. Jake has taken his shirt off and is sitting slumped against the pillows. He is holding between his thumb and forefinger the black chip worth ten thousand pounds from Eden and is staring at it reflectively. His hair has fallen over his forehead and he looks up at me slowly. At that moment he doesn't look drunk. Just devastated. Utterly devastated.

I stand frozen in the doorway.

It is impossible to tell what he is thinking. He takes a drag of his cigarette and blows it out slowly. He puts the chip on the side table and

turns toward me. 'Come in,' he invites softly. 'Because I'm dying to fuck you with my tongue.'

'That's so dirty,' I say as I discard my skirt on the way to the four-poster. I climb onto the mattress, take the cigarette out of his mouth, kill it at the bottom of the glass, and position myself with my sex right slap bang on his mouth.

My back arches as he begins to devour me. I come quickly and intensely. When I look down into his eyes, they are almost black with desire. Leaning back I slowly rub my hand over his crotch. I pull my body away from his face and I start to take his trousers off.

'I need to take a piss. Don't go anywhere,' he says.

I listen to the strong splash of his urine hitting the toilet bowl and I remember my nan saying, 'You can tell a man's health by the strength of his morning piss.' Well, it's confirmed. He's one healthy man. I hear the tap running and then he comes back. There is still a little sway in his walk, but he seems more sober now.

He stands at the edge of the bed looking at me. 'Every time I see that sexy little mouth of yours I just want to fuck it. I want to fuck it until it is all red and swollen and then I want to fuck it some more.'

And that is exactly what he does after he picks up the phone and cancels my taxi. He puts the phone down and fucks my mouth long

and deep and then he finishes off in my pussy. There is no tenderness given and none asked. This is just lust. Pure lust. Both of us craving each other's bodies and taking it hard and fast because we can't have what we really want. At least that is true for me. What I want is shimmering in the distance. Way beyond my reach.

Afterward he lies beside me. I can see that the alcohol is shutting him down. He is valiantly fighting it, but the edge of a deep sleep is less than a blink away.

'You're going to have one hell of a hangover when you wake up.'

'I'll live,' he mutters.

'Go to sleep, Jake,' I encourage.

'Will you be here when I wake up?'

I pause. 'Yeah.'

'Don't leave me, Lily, or Jewel, or whatever your real name is.'

'My real name is Lily Strom,' I whisper.

His eyes widen. 'No, your name is Lily Eden,' he murmurs.

I smile sadly, and he runs his fingertips along the curve of my hip. My body quivers at the delicate touch. My nipples come alive, hardening, darkening, tingling, calling. I stop thinking about anything else but him and the strong sensation that he is touching my very soul. The emotion is unbearably intense, maybe too intense. A tear leaks out of each corner of my eyes.

No matter how many obstacles, our bodies can always find each other. My brain says no, but my body tells me this man has to be part of my future. I have to find a way for us to be together. And staying here while I am confused and vulnerable is not the way. I need time to sort out what I am going to do about Mills, my job and my terrible guilt about the love I have for this man.

He stops stroking my hip and drags his thumb down the path of my tears. I swallow hard and blink. He puts his thumb into his mouth.

'Salty,' he pronounces.

I flash a wobbly smile.

'Did you know that otters hold hands before they go to sleep so they don't float away?'

I slip my hand into his and he tightens his hold on it.

He smiles and his eyelids droop. He forces them open. It's a lost battle. Not long to go now.

'The first time I saw you I thought you were an angel come to save me,' he mumbles.

I say nothing, I just watch as he slips into a deep drunken stupor. I lie next to him for another few minutes watching him, listening to his even breathing. When his body is totally relaxed and dead to the world I slowly pull my hand out of his grip, but even though his entire body is limp as if passed from this world, his hand is clinging onto me like a claw. Gently, one by one I pry his fingers away. Very gently I kiss his forehead.

Quietly I get out of bed and into my skirt. I retrieve my panties from the pocket of his pants and go into the living room. On hotel stationery I write a note.

> *I'm not running away.*
> *I just need a bit of time*
> *to think and sort my head*
> *out.*
> *xx Lily*

Then I softly close the door. I have a plane to catch. I am in such a daze that it is only when I am high in the sky that I realize I am still wearing both my engagement and wedding rings. I twist them around my finger in horror. I can't believe I have left him. My body feels hollow where my heart should be.

FOUR

Lily

I clear customs in Heathrow and head straight for the payphones. I find one that is coin operated and lay my coins in a row along the metal ledge. I lift the receiver, pick up a pound, push it into the slot, and dial Robin's number. His answering service clicks on and for a split second it occurs to me that I have done the wrong thing. In that split second I even consider terminating the call without saying anything, but then I hear myself speak.

'Hey, Robin. No panic. Everything is just fine. Just touching base. Saying hello. Call you another day. Byeeee.'

I click the disconnect button quickly and close my eyes, full of regret, wishing I hadn't called him. That was another mistake. My voice had been normal, cheery even, but while I was talking an announcement had been made. He will know I am calling from an airport and, being the bright button that he is, alarm bells will be going off as to why if all is well I would be calling him from an airport simply to say hello. With every decision I take I seem to be digging myself deeper and deeper into a hole.

On the spur of the moment I decide not to go back to the company flat, and instead take a taxi to my grandmother's house. Staring unhappily out of the window I fret about whether to call my mother. I know I should, but ever since Luke died, she has become so fragile I have learned to either bear my burdens silently or take them over to Nan.

The driver drops me off outside her ground floor flat, and I go up to her blue door and ring the bell. Her little face appears at the window. I wave and she breaks into a massive grin. At that moment she is no longer a sprightly seventy-two-year-old woman, but a mere child.

In seconds her beaming face is at her open door.

She greets me in the traditional Chinese way, by asking me if I have eaten.

'Yes,' I reply automatically, but she bundles me energetically through the door past the Feng Shui cat with its waving arm, and into her small, rather dim kitchen. It has old-fashioned, dark wood furniture and the air smells of incense that has been lit in the red prayer altar of the Kitchen God, Zao Jun. In front of his statue she has left an offering: a blue bowl of oranges.

'Sit, sit,' Nan says, and starts filling her electric steamer with water.

'I'm actually not hungry,' I protest.

'You're never hungry,' she grumbles. She switches on the appliance and turns around, her hands on her hips. 'Look at you, as thin as one of those throw-away chopsticks.' She narrows her eyes. 'And have you been lying in the sun again?'

'It's called a tan, Nan.'

'Tan, my foot. These unattractive Western traditions that you have picked up. You should have seen your great-grandmother. She was as white as a lotus blossom.'

'Talking of traditions, didn't she also have bound feet?'

She stares at me disapprovingly. 'What's that got to do with taking care of your skin?'

'Nan,' I say tiredly, 'I haven't come here to talk about the state of my skin.'

She shakes her head and moves toward her freezer. She rummages around and brings out white buns made of Hong Kong flour with chicken and pork filling. She shows me the packet. 'See? Your favorite brand.'

'Thanks,' I say weakly. The last thing I feel like is food.

While she busies herself placing the buns into the steamer I look around me. Nothing in Nan's kitchen ever seems to change. From the time Luke and I were kids everything looks and smells the same. We used to love coming here. There was always some kind of celebration— moon cake festival, lanterns, Chinese New Year festivities when we used to eat sticky sweet cakes, get money in red packets, and burn fire crackers to speed the Kitchen God on his journey back to heaven.

Nan wipes her hands and comes to sit beside me.

'Nan,' I begin. 'You know I became an undercover police officer, right?'

'Of course. You told me this yourself. I'm not senile yet, you know?'

'Well, anyway, I was sent on this assignment and...er...'

Her sharp dark eyes gaze at me curiously.

'I think I've developed, well, feelings for my target.'

There is no discernible expression in her face. 'Tell me about him. What kind of man is he?'

'He is loyal to his family, kind to animals, and... He is fair.'

'Why do the police want him?'

'He's supposed to be a drug dealer.'

I see fear whip into her eyes and she clasps her hands tightly together.

'But I don't think he is one, though.'

Her hands unclasp with relief.

I bite my lip. 'But I am also afraid that my judgment may be colored by the way I feel about him.'

She leans forward. 'Can it be the police have got it wrong?'

'Unlikely,' I admit reluctantly.

She frowns and studies me. 'So why have you come to see me then?'

For a moment I stare into her familiar eyes. And then I realize that I have come to see her because I trust her. I trust her not to bullshit me about anything. And because I know she is non-judgmental, except about things like getting a tan and modern Western ways. But more importantly because I know that something is wrong. If I put it all out on the table for her to peer at she might pick up what I have missed.

'I've come because I'm feeling confused and guilty. And I know you can't make it better, but maybe just talking about it all to you will clear it up for me.'

'What are you feeling guilty about?'

'I believe I am betraying Luke in the worst possible way by falling in love with a suspected drug dealer. Even if the police are wrong, and that is a very unlikely scenario, it is still all a horrible, horrible mess. I feel as if I have become so steeped in filth and mire that a part of me will never get out of it.'

Nan leans forward. 'When you were born I wanted your mother to name you Lotus, but she refused. She said that name was too old-fashioned. In an attempt at compromise she named you Lily, but she didn't understand. She thought because my name, Lan, means orchid, I wanted you to be named after a flower too. I didn't. I wanted to call you Lotus because I looked into your big blue eyes and I felt the sheer strength and purity of your personality. My granddaughter is going to grow up to be strong and pure. Like the Lotus she can remain in filth and mire all her life but she will rise out of it clean and pure. Not a tiny drop of mud or slime can stick to her.'

Tears fill my eyes. I blink them away quickly. 'I don't feel very pure, Nan. In fact I feel as if my feelings for Jake and my guilt about betraying Luke are clouding my instincts and intellect, and making me miss something. Something very important.'

She covers my hand with one of hers. 'When you were a baby, not even two years old, I would sit you on that cabinet.' She points to the high, lacquered cabinet where she stores her odds and ends. 'And I would tell you not to move. And you wouldn't. You wouldn't move at all. You'd sit there with your legs dangling down.'

I look at the cabinet. It does seem a high perch to put a small child on.

'It was amazing how you were aware of the danger, but unafraid. I could even leave the room. I did a few times too. But I could never do that with Luke. I could never trust him. I always knew he didn't know what was good for him. You have to trust your instincts. If you think he is a good man, then I trust you. If your instincts are telling you something is not right then I would trust them implicitly.'

I nod gratefully. I know Nan is right. The only times I have gone wrong in my life are when I have not followed my instincts.

'There is something else, too, that is really bothering me. I am so in love with him I can't imagine my life without him, but I don't know whether he really cares about me, or if it's just sex for him.'

Nan's eyes flash. 'A man can find sex anywhere.'

'Yes, but not the kind of sex we have. We can't keep our hands off each other.'

'Intimacy is the flesh clearing the path for hearts and souls,' she says primly.

'What happens if the lust goes and there is no love?'

'Wait here,' Nan commands, and goes into the hallway. I hear her enter her bedroom and open her armoire. She comes back with a small box. Seashells have been crudely stuck all around it. She puts it on the table in front of me, sits down and looks at me.

'Go on, open it,' she invites.

I do and it is full of an assortment of small, worthless objects, a yellow button, a bit of shiny foil, a bright orange earring, a screw... I raise my eyes back to her. 'What are all these things?'

'Don't you remember them at all?'

I frown. Vaguely. Something...almost dream-like breaks into my memory. I pick up the orange earring. It is smooth and old. I look up at her. 'I remember this. I know it's mine, but I don't remember where it came from or how it slots into my past.'

She smiles.

'Yes, these are all yours. From the time you were about three years old until you were five you lived with Granddad and me in a rented house close to an abandoned factory. Many crows lived there. At first they would swoop down and eat the food that you accidentally dropped. But then you began to feed them, nuts, breadcrumbs, dry dog food. And they began to bring you presents. All these were brought to you by the crows. They were showing you their love.'

'I don't remember,' I say with a frown.

'It was a long time ago.'

And suddenly I have a memory, of a flock of crows on the ground beside me. They are all busy feeding. I smile at Nan full of wonder. 'I remember them now. Why did you show me this today?'

'Bright shiny things are given to us by people who love us.' She looks at my rings. 'Like those.'

'You noticed?'

'I'm old. I'm not blind,' she says, and goes to take the buns out of the steamer.

I sigh. 'Yeah, we got married. I'm afraid it's all a huge mess.'

'Never mind. Let's eat now. What is this thing the British are always saying? It will all come out in the wash.'

'Nan, why did Luke and I come to live with you?'

Nan doesn't turn to look at me. 'Your mother was ill at that time.'

'She didn't want us, did she?'

She whirls around suddenly, her face as fierce as I have ever seen it. 'She wanted both of you, but she was ill, Lily. She was ill, the same way Luke was.'

There is so much I don't know about my own family, but I am learning. Finally, the pieces are falling into place. I understand now why Luke and I always felt like outsiders. Our mother rejected us even when we were babies. No wonder I am so afraid of love. And perhaps it was why Luke turned to drugs. There is something missing inside us.

When Nan puts the buns in front of me I realize that I am actually starving. I hardly ate on the plane and I haven't eaten a proper meal since my dinner at Shanghai Lily.

That night I stay over in Nan's house. Uncle Seng, an old friend, comes for dinner and we eat noodle soup with fishballs and Kitato playing in the background. Uncle Seng is funny and Nan laughs a lot. It gives me time to lean back in my chair, sip my white tea, and feel the loss of Jake by my side. Uncle Seng leaves early and I go into the kitchen to wash up. I tell Nan to relax, but she comes and helps to dry the dishes.

'You must be tired. You better go to bed,' she says, hanging up the towel.

'Yes, I suppose I am. Goodnight, Nan. Thank you for today,' I say and bend to kiss her.

'You won't tell your mother I put you on the cabinet, will you?' she asks.

I laugh. 'Why did you do it, anyway?'

'Because you used to look so cute and solemn up there.'

'Oh, Nan, how I love you,' I whisper, and hug her small delicate frame tightly. Her rib bones seem so small and birdlike.

'Sleep well, little Lotus.'

I climb into my old bed and fall asleep almost immediately. I dream of the crows. They come bearing gifts. Their unrelieved blackness is neither startling nor offensive. I open my arms and receive them gladly. They are my special friends from another time.

FIVE

Lily

I left my keys to Jake's house in his suitcase before I left the Hard Rock Hotel, which means I won't be able to let myself into his house if he is not in. Fortunately, standing across the road from the house I see that his car is parked close by but in a different place from when we left for Vegas. So I know not only that he is back, but also that he is in. I do not know what kind of reception I am going to get, but I know he won't turn me away.

His body won't let him.

Maybe that is why I have not called first. Calling would mean our bodies don't get to talk. I cross the road. At the bottom of the steps I stop, courage suddenly deserting me. It is startling just how nervous I am. My organs feel like they are floating inside a hollow space. I take a deep breath. I think I am afraid of what he will be like without the alcohol.

Come on, Lily, just a few steps more. You've come this far. It's not like you ran out on him or anything like that. You left a note. You just needed a bit of time to think.

I look up at the sky. It is a hazy white.

I want to take those last few steps and ring the bell. I want to see him again, but I am terrified I will see a stranger with cold, mean eyes. I debate the matter. What's the worst that can happen? He slams the door in my face. A small voice speaks, *I'm not prepared for that. I can't go back to what I was when I lost Luke.* This is a bad idea. Maybe I should leave and then call first. Prepare him. My body starts turning to walk away when in my peripheral vision the curtain twitches. Oh God in heaven! He has seen me.

It galvanizes me. I don't want him thinking I'm a coward. I run lightly up the stairs and ring the bell.

The door opens almost instantly and my voice dies in my throat. My eyes widen with shock and I feel my soul shrivel. This I had not prepared for.

'Well, well, look what the cat dragged in,' Andrea Mornington drawls as her eyes travel down my body derisively, while she stands in Jake's fucking shirt! The buttons have not even been done up. She has just thrown it over her naked body and is clutching the edges together. Underneath the shirt her legs are long and bare and her toenails are painted a pretty peach.

Fuck him.

He went back to her!

Just like that.

The sensation of shock is so immense that I feel physically ill. I want to vomit. I am jealous,

horribly jealous of her standing in my man's shirt. At that moment I don't think of what I have done to him or how I have betrayed him. I just feel betrayed. Utterly and completely. I really believed we had something rare and special. A kind of deep connection that I have not had with another human being.

Her eyes note my suffering with great satisfaction. There is not an ounce of pity in them. I see her clearly then. She has never in her life sung the song of pain, or had the branches torn from her tree. She is one of those lucky women. Bestowed with everything.

I open my mouth and no words come out!

'It's always a good idea to call first,' she advises insolently.

It is not rage I feel but pain. Such pain that I don't want to punch her, or scratch her eyes out. I just want to run away somewhere no one will see me and howl in pain.

Some part of me refuses to believe what I am seeing. What if she is tricking me? What if he is not in? I force the words out.

'Is he in?'

'Obviously,' she says, with an amused smirk.

I won't scratch your smug, spoilt face, but I'll leave you with this: 'Tell him... Tell him his wife was here.'

Without waiting to see her reaction I whirl away from her, and lurch toward the steps. But my legs are so unsteady that I miss the first step and, with arms flailing and an involuntary cry starting at the back of my throat, I begin

flying face first toward the hard, concrete pavement below.

Oh shit! Now she will witness my utter humiliation, too.

My descent is stopped suddenly by an iron hand. Wet and strong, it curls itself around my forearm and jerks me backwards. The force is so great I slam into a hard wall of solid muscles running with water droplets. The clean smell of soap and shampoo envelops me.

In a daze I feel myself being pulled through the entrance past an open-mouthed Andrea. I turn my shocked face to the owner of the hand. His hair is plastered to his head and rivulets of water are still running down his face and neck. My stunned brain makes a mental note: he was in the shower. His only covering is a small, white towel slung around his delectable hips. He must have just pulled the first thing that came to his hand, and run down the stairs when he heard the doorbell.

Did he know it was me ringing?

He propels me into the living room, and keeping a firm hold of my hand turns to glare at Andrea. She has followed us in and is standing at the door watching. An odd, unfathomable expression crosses his face. He shakes his head slightly to himself, part irritation, part exasperation.

'Get back into your own clothes and leave, Andrea,' he says tightly.

'What about lunch?' she asks sulkily.

'What about lunch?' It is obvious that he is finding it difficult to keep his temper in check.

'You promised to take me.'

'And I will, *another time*... If you get out of here right now.'

Huffily, but with impressive flamboyance, she flings his shirt to the floor and in her underwear stalks to a sofa where her clothes are. The bitch! She had wanted me to think she was naked underneath Jake's shirt. That I had interrupted them at an intimate moment. Jake turns his gaze back to me. I have so many questions eating at me, but I am too frozen to say anything. My mouth is still hanging open.

I clamp it shut—I can wait until she is gone before I go ape shit.

She shoots daggers at me before bestowing a fake, happy smile on Jake. 'See you later, then,' she calls and flounces out of the room.

We hear the door close and Jake says in a weary voice, 'Don't make me come there and put you out, Andrea.'

There is a muffled sound of outrage and then the door slams hard.

'How did you know she hadn't gone?'

'When things don't go Andrea's way she tends to slam doors.'

My mind is a seething mess of emotions. How dare he? How dare he act so cool?

'What was she doing here?'

'When she came I was training. I went to take a shower. She was supposed to wait...in her own clothes.'

I still don't like it. She obviously feels she has some sort of hold on him. And what is that thing about taking her out to lunch? But I can't act all jealous. Now is not the time. We have other far more important things to talk about.

I gaze at him, and suddenly I am aware that he is standing in an inadequately small towel. And he is staring at my mouth. Heat is coming off him in waves. My gaze leaves his smoldering eyes and skitters down to his throat.

'I'm glad you came,' he murmurs.

'Why?' The sound is strangled. His nearness is doing things to me. We have been apart for so little time and yet, it feels as if it has been ages since I have had him inside me.

'Because it's saved me the trouble of going down to Vauxhall to fetch your ass back here.'

My eyes rush up to his. 'You know where I live?'

'There are two things wrong with you, princess. You're too naïve for your own good, and you're always wearing too many fucking clothes.' His voice is low and husky and he watches me like a hungry beast.

I flush and feel wetness pool between my legs. The air around us is thick with all kinds of emotion.

'Um, yeah, we really need to talk, Jake.'

'Everything in good time, but first...' In an admirably smooth movement he unbuttons, unzips and pulls my jeans down my legs. 'I've got to have you.' Sitting on his haunches, his

mouth is so close to my sex I feel his breath as warm puffs of air through my panties. I take a shaky breath. Mother of God, this man is something else. I rest my palms on the thick knots of strong muscles on his shoulders as he slides my panties down to the floor. I step out of them.

'We really should talk first,' I whisper without any conviction.

'Aren't you even a little bit keen to have my cock inside you?'

'Not really,' I gasp.

'You're dripping, babe.'

'You're an asshole, Jake.'

He grins, his eyes flashing.

My breasts feel heavy, my nipples hard and hungry. *Should I be doing this?* my mind tries to reason fleetingly, but it is gone when he sticks a thick finger inside me. 'Oh,' I cry.

'Oh, indeed,' he says and standing up, walks me backwards until I am pushed up against a wall. He whips that ridiculously inadequate towel off his bronzed body and throws it to the ground. I have only a flash of him in all his erect glory before my right thigh is grabbed and hoisted up. I wrap it around his hard waist. This is where I belong. I am back where I belong. He drags his fingers along my crack, already slick with juices.

'I can't wait to feel your sweet pussy around my cock,' he says softly, as his thumb massages my clit knowing that the light caresses will drive me insane.

'Fucking give it to her then,' I snarl.

He laughs softly and forces his shaft up into me.

'Oh God!' I whimper, staring up at him. Jesus, how I've missed having this thick pillar of meat buried deep inside me. The fullness of him is perfect. Absolutely perfect.

His eyes blaze into mine.

Utterly drunk on the look in his eyes, I groan. Possibly because I have come to accept that I love him and will do everything in my power to keep him, it is more satisfying than at any other time.

He rams into me relentlessly, until my supporting leg begins to twitch with tension. I fear my leg is about to give way under me.

'I can't take it anymore,' I gasp, my sex clenching like crazy.

'Yes, you can,' he says. 'Remember I *own* your pussy. She starts when I start and she stops when I stop.' He swats my ass hard, the sound is loud and meaty, and pounds me even harder. Pain blurs into pleasure. My leg buckles and I wind both legs around his thighs and my hands around his neck and hang there, trembling. His hands come around to grip my bare buttocks and hold me in place.

'Jaaaake... I'm coming,' I warn.

'No,' he snarls. 'You come when I tell you to fucking come.'

'I can't wait,' I moan desperately.

'Yes, you can,' he bites out and pushes his tongue into my mouth. I suck on it greedily. I

45

can feel the rush beginning to take hold of my muscles, and I strain to hold it back. My pulse pounds in my ears and between my legs so hard that my body starts vibrating with the intense effort of holding back the oncoming climax.

'Let me come,' I cry harshly.

'Come,' he commands, and I plunge, trembling, twisting, jerking, into a void that is more vast and fantastic than the night sky while my hands grip him hard and close to my body through the splendor of his own orgasm.

SIX

Lily

Breathing heavily and with his eyes closed, he leans his forehead against mine. I feel his wet hair tickling my skin and his cock still spurting his seed inside me. Suddenly, he opens his lids and I am staring into the starburst of his eyes. This close, they are beautiful gems that have the ability to see right into my soul. I feel naked. All my secrets laid bare. *Do you know about Luke, Jake? Do you know why I was willing to betray you?*

He raises his head, gently pulls out of me, and unhooks my legs from his thighs and sets me back on my own two feet. Very shakily I lean against the wall and look up at him.

'Are you purposely being succulent?' he teases.

I shake my head. I can't say anything. My throat has closed over. He leans forward and bites my mouth. I reach down and rub his glistening cock. He starts kissing me, no, not kissing, devouring me. It is rough and it is possessive. I rewrap my hands around his neck and the empty ache between my legs starts again. I want him back inside me. And I know exactly how to do it. I pull away from his mouth and drop to my knees.

With him I am a dirty girl. Nothing is taboo. All is allowed.

He rests his palms on the wall at shoulder level and throws his head back as I hold his semi-hard shaft by the base and swirl the tip of my tongue around the crown. Languorously, I lap up the shaft as if I am licking ice cream melting down a cone on a summer's day. Then I suck it voraciously, as if it is a massive, muscular tongue. I swallow it halfway... Then I take it so deep into my throat, a growl smolders in his throat. The sound is so damn hot, it's sinful. It shivers onto my skin, scattering goose bumps wherever it touches. God knows how long I suck him because my lips have become numb, but I do get him rock hard.

I slide him out of my mouth and look up at him, my lips parted.

He looks down at me with naked hunger. Mother of God! His eyes are almost lime! I want him. No, I need him. I stare back, my eyes speaking a language of their own. Cock. Dick. Hard. Delicious. Ready. You. Get inside me.

'Fuck my mouth,' I whisper, but it comes out harsh and throaty. I fit him back, hard and thick, between my lips. A hand slides into my hair. Clenches. Tugs. But this is not me submitting. This is me at full power. This is me entirely in control. Me deciding. Me being greedy. Because I already know exactly what he is going to do.

He is Mr. Generous. I *never* come away with nothing.

He begins to thrust. Softly first then harder and harder—enough to see me gag and choke. Then he comes out of me, and grabbing me by the waist, picks me up as if I weigh no more than a feather. He puts me face down over the armrest of the sofa. Shivering with anticipation, my ass in the air, I twist back to watch.

He opens my legs wide and looks at my bare ass and my sex, open and smeared with sex juices. Glossy, swollen, needy. For a second his eyes rise up to mine. What is in his eyes is pure, unadulterated possession. I get it immediately. My sex belongs to him. And only him. Woe betide any man who comes between him and me.

With a wild cry, he grabs my hips and plunges into me. He is branding me. With an answering cry, I push back into him. It is crude, it is primitive. It is what we both are. His skin slaps against mine as he fucks me so hard I feel the leather of the sofa chafe against my thighs.

With the solid heat of his body pressed against me I feel strangely safe. As if the outside world with all its problems and demands does not exist.

'With you the burn never dissipates, even slightly,' I whisper.

49

'I'm glad,' he mutters. 'Because I wish I could tie you to my bed with your legs wide open so I could come and bury my tongue or my cock inside you any time I please.'

Considering how hard and intensely passionate we have been, it surprises me when I feel my cheeks burn.

He strokes me with the back of his finger. 'What a strange little thing you are. Big-eyed innocence and—'

The word innocence pulls me out of my languor. And suddenly the air between us changes. I start to wriggle under him. He rises and pulls out of me. My sprawled position feels awkward and embarrassing. His seed is leaking out of me. I try to right myself, but he puts a restraining hand on the small of my back.

'Don't hide from me, Lil. Just relax,' he says. There is husky control in his voice, and I cease all movement. He picks up the towel he discarded earlier and kneeling at the apex of my spread thighs tenderly wipes my swollen sex. After the rough fucking his touch is so gentle I am surprised.

'I love your pussy. It is so beautiful,' he murmurs and plants a kiss right on my core, making my stomach clench.

Then he opens my flesh wide and whispers something into my sex. Hazily, I hear my name, but I cannot make the rest of the sentence out.

He cannot not have feelings for me. It is impossible. He must care some. Nan is right.

He cares. He must. I can't even imagine the alternative. He pushes his tongue into me and gently licks me. As if he were a cat or dog cleaning its baby.

'More,' I whisper feverishly. 'Fill me up, Jake. I am so empty without you.'

He pushes a thick finger into me. 'You're not empty, Lil. I'm here.'

He plays with me, never-ending circles, until I feel my back arching. 'I think I'm coming. Can I come?'

'Yes.'

The sensation is so intense, so wild, I try to pull away, but he tightens his hold and makes me submit. I climax with my slick clit inside his hot mouth.

He stands, closes my legs into some semblance of respectability and pulls me up. Our eyes meet. God! This man is so beautiful.

'You look like you could do with a drink,' he says, tying the towel around his hips.

I find my jeans and pull them on. He walks to the bar, pours us a glass of whiskey each. He passes me a glass and our fingers touch. A spark goes through me. I withdraw my hand, spilling whiskey. His eyes are dark, but I can tell by the set of his mouth that the sex is over. It is time to talk.

I pour the whiskey into my throat. It burns all the way down.

He raises his eyebrows, but says nothing. I notice that he doesn't drink, but puts his glass down on the counter. He swivels his head.

'You wanted to talk?'

'Yeah.'

Suddenly I am nervous. What if it is only sex with him? What if Nan is wrong? I swallow hard. I open my mouth and his phone rings. He frowns. I have noticed that his phone almost never rings. The last time it rang it had been Dom telling him about the fire.

'Can you wait one moment?'

I nod.

He moves toward it. Looks at the screen and immediately presses the answer button.

'Yeah,' he says and his voice is worried.

I can hear a woman's voice. It sounds panicked and hysterical.

'Calm down. Calm down,' he says.

The voice becomes slightly subdued.

'Yes, it's true,' he admits.

And the voice screams so loud he stares at the phone in disbelief. Then he looks at me and silently mouths, 'It's my mother.'

I nod solemnly. A family problem of some kind, obviously.

'Look, Ma. I'll come around tonight. Just please calm down. I'll explain everything when I get there, OK?'

Even from where I am I can hear her ranting, not in the least comforted. At one point Jake has to hold the phone away from his ear.

'What the hell are you on about? I'm perfectly fine.' He runs his hand through his hair distractedly.

'All right, I'll be there in less than an hour,' he concedes.

I hear another explosion of sound.

'OK, OK, I'll leave now. I'll be there in fifteen minutes.'

I hear quiet sobbing.

'Ma, stop it. Ma?'

I hear another hysterical outpouring.

He sighs with frustration. 'I'll come right now, OK? Just wait for me.'

He terminates the call and looks at me. 'She's a *bit* distraught.'

'What happened?'

'Apparently, Andrea called and told her I married you.' He raises an eyebrow. 'Any idea how Andrea knew?'

'Oops, sorry,' I say, biting my bottom lip.

He grins at me. 'It's not like I wasn't going to tell her anyway, but it does mean I have to go see her now. Will you wait for me here? We'll talk when I come back.'

I nod.

'Come upstairs and keep me company while I dress.'

'Yeah?'

'Yeah.'

And I thought it was going to be difficult and awkward. It is not. I smile. God! I'm so in love with this man. 'OK.'

I watch him pull on a pair of black jeans in silence, just drinking in the sight of him. He pulls a black T-shirt over his taut muscles.

'Why does your mother hate me?'

He looks at me seriously and doesn't try to gloss over the issue. 'I don't know. But I know she doesn't know you the way I do and when she does she'll absolutely love you...' For a moment it seems as if the sentence is not complete, then he smiles and goes to the door. I follow him.

At the door he turns and kisses me.

'You smell of sex and me,' he whispers in my ear.

I rear back. 'I'll have a shower before you get back.'

'Don't you dare. I love it.' A smile tilts his mouth and warmth kindles in my belly. He goes down the steps, turns back and starts walking backwards mouthing, 'Be back soon. Don't go anywhere.'

He blows a kiss and I shyly return it. Maybe, it's going to be all right.

I watch him get into his car and drive off. Then I close the door and lean against it. The house is large and deathly quiet around me. I shut my eyes and hold to the fierce joy that burns in my chest. I think of the way his gaze had followed my tongue as it licked my lower lip. I remember the heat and I recall the tenderness between us, almost surreal. And I cover my mouth to hide the smile of pure happiness.

And what do the gods do?

They make my phone ring. I look at it and for a few rings I do nothing. Just stare at the number. I knew I shouldn't have called Robin. Then I press Answer and put it to my ear.

A woman says cheerily, 'Hey, Lily. It's Amber.'

'Hey, Amber,' I say automatically. Amber is the way that Robin makes contact with me.

'How are you?'

'Fine.' I clear my throat. 'I'm fine.'

'We should meet. Go out for coffee or something.'

'OK. Where do you want to go?'

'How about Starbucks? You like the green tea thingamajig there, don't you?'

'Yes, I love it. Let's meet there. When?'

'How about now?'

'Now?'

'Yes, I have so much to tell you.'

'Right. I'll be there in the next twenty minutes.'

'Oh, good. Can't wait to see you again.'

'Same here,' I reply.

'Bye,' she says in a high, bright voice.

'Bye,' I say in a low, sad voice.

You take your aim. You fire. And shoot me down. Fuck you, Fate.

My legs feel like lead. I go into Jake's office. I have only been here once. I know the drawers are all locked and the desk is always stunningly bare. I take a piece of paper from the printer.

I take the quill from the ink stand. Just like him to have a fucking quill instead of a ballpoint pen. I feel the tears pricking at my eyes. No, I will not cry. There is a way out. I

know it. I am unlucky but he is lucky and he will get what he wants. And he wants me. I know that. Well, I think I know that. Maybe he doesn't love me. But he wants me. I can tell. With every action he shows me. And Jake always gets what he wants.

I write my note. It is short and to the point.

Jake,
I have to go out for a bit. I'll see you when I get back, OK? x

Should I add another kiss? One seems so informal. A jeering voice says, *WTF!* So I add three more kisses.

And then I leave my sanctuary.

SEVEN

Lily

The Starbucks in Baker Street is quiet. Robin is sitting on a sofa in a corner at the back. He stands and waves to me. I walk toward him. He is wearing jeans and an expensive leather jacket over a Ralph Lauren T-shirt. His face is familiar—his eyes travel my face and body quickly, assessing, assimilating. I can see that he hasn't ordered anything yet.

'Look at you,' he says loudly, so that anyone watching would just think we are friends meeting after a long time.

He kisses me on the cheeks enthusiastically while I stand awkwardly in the loose circle of his arm. 'How've you been?'

'Fine.'

'What will you have?'

'A latte.'

'Anything to eat?'

I shake my head.

'You sure? The company is picking up the bill,' he tempts with a grin.

'Not hungry, Rob,' I reply.

'Right,' he says in a more serious tone, and goes off to the serving counter. I look around me. There are only two other customers in this back section—a woman scrolling through the messages on her handheld and a man who is immersed in a newspaper. I turn away and stare at my handbag. There is no queue and Robin is back quickly. He places my latte in front of me. He is drinking a cappuccino.

'Thanks,' I say, reaching for two sugar sachets. I tear them and upend them into my coffee.

He sits and does the same.

Then he looks around him casually again, sees what I saw and lets his eyes come back to me, his face creased into lines of concern. 'Lily, what the hell is going on? Why did you initiate contact from an airport?' he asks in a low, urgent tone.

I take a deep breath. ''Cause I fucking need your help, Robin,' I choke.

'Jesus,' he says. 'Oh fuck!'

I close my eyes.

'Is that a fucking engagement ring on your finger?' he asks.

It is hard to tell at a glance since the stone on the engagement ring is so big that there is another plain band there. 'Yeah, and a wedding ring,' I say.

His mouth opens. 'You better start from the beginning,' he says cautiously.

I have a speech prepared. 'I...er...um... I... Well...uh...ah...um... Fuck, Robin, I went and slept with him and now it's all a mess.'

He exhales audibly. 'Look, it doesn't matter. You're not the first agent who has slept with their target. Just, well, just keep your feelings separate.'

The way a prostitute does, I think, and suddenly I realize I can't talk to him. I can't tell him anything. Not a thing. Calling him was definitely a mistake. He doesn't know that I am bonded with Jake. He doesn't know that I would die for Jake.

Robin's back straightens suddenly and his expression changes into one of alarm. 'Fuck it, Lily, he's here,' he says. He forces his expression back into one of normality and leans back into the leather couch.

I freeze.

'Anyway, did you know that Andy's wife has just had a baby?' he says.

I want to reply. I want to be normal but I can't.

'Nine pounds, the nipper was,' he adds, smiling.

I open and close my mouth like a demented fish.

And then the seat next to me depresses and I feel my life spiraling out of control. Slowly, I turn my head and feel a stab of pain in my gut. Jake is *nothing* like the man I know. I stare at him in perfect astonishment. His eyes are like green ice. Impenetrable. He does not spare me a glance. He has locked eyes with Robin. Hostility and animosity come off him in waves that you can feel and almost touch.

'Introduce me, then, Lily,' he says silkily, his eyes blazing.

I sit frozen. Unable to utter a single word.

Robin is one cool customer. 'I'm an old classmate of Lily's. We just bumped into each other. I should be going, really. The wife is waiting at the supermarket,' he smiles. His smile is just right. His manner is just right, but Jake doesn't buy it.

'What are you? Her handler?'

Robin's look of incredulity is not faked.

'What?' he says. 'Look, mate, I don't know what you're talking about, but I'm not getting involved. We're just old friends. I was getting a coffee and I saw Lily. That's it. I'm off.' He starts to stand.

'Yes, run away, but if I see you around her again, I swear I'll break every fucking bone in your body.' Jake smiles. The smile is pure menace. Why did I think I knew him? I know only the tip of the iceberg. I remember Shane saying, 'Do you think he treats everyone the way he treats you?' I stare at him, amazed.

Robin is on his feet, his hands raised, palms showing. 'Look, mate, I don't want no trouble.'

'Fuck off, then.'

Robin's eyes bounce to me. I nod quickly, and he leaves.

Jake turns to look at me. 'You want to play undercover detective? Be my guest, I can play

the fool for you, but if I ever fucking see you meet him or any other man behind my back again you'll have to watch me fucking kill the cunt,' he snarls.

'Robin is my go-between.'

'I don't care what the fuck he is. You want to meet him? Tell me first.'

It's so fucked up it's unreal. He doesn't care if I want to spy on him, he just doesn't want me to do it behind his back. It would be laughable if it was not so weird. The only thing I can think of doing is using what has always worked. I touch his groin. Mistake. Big mistake. He grabs my hand, so hard I gasp.

'Don't, Lil. Don't degrade what we have.'

He lets go of my hand suddenly. I rub it. 'How did you know I was here?'

'How do you think?'

My eyes widen. 'What? You're having me followed?'

'Yes.' He says it like it is the most natural thing in the world to spy on your girlfriend or wife.

'Why?' I breathe. Too shocked to be angry.

'Because you got beat up by a pervert. Because I care. Take your fucking pick, Lil.'

I shake my head as if to clear it. 'And what about Andrea?'

His turn to frown. 'What about her?'

'Didn't I hear you arrange to meet her for lunch?' I ask, sarcasm dripping from my voice.

'Andrea is an old family friend. She takes care of my house when I am away. She picks

the mail up from the floor and makes sure that no pipes have burst et cetera. I pay her for that. She's nothing to me.'

'Well, it doesn't seem like that from where I'm sitting.'

He frowns. 'What does it seem like to you?'

'It seems that she is in love with you.'

'Andrea is not in love with me. She's got her hook in the water for a rich man. And she knows the score with me.'

'Her behavior today was not that of someone who knows the score,' I remind.

He shrugs carelessly. 'All right, I'll hire someone else.'

'Good,' I say as nonchalantly as I can, but inside all my cells are coming alive with joy: Not only do I never need to see her snooty, insolent face again, but I won't have to worry about their relationship anymore either.

I look at his beautiful face. Even in a public place all I want to do is rub my body against his. I turn away and look at my untouched latte and Robin's cappuccino. 'Are you not afraid I will uncover something that will send you to prison?'

'No,' he says shortly.

'Why?'

'Because, Lily, my dearest, for the past ten years I have extricated myself and my organization from almost all that is illegal. I've nothing to fear.'

'What about that bed of money then?' I challenge.

'Protection money.'

I frown. 'You don't need to collect protection money.'

'It's true, I don't need it. It is one of the last bastions of an organization that I want to give up, but it would mean abandoning Eden and Dom's clubs to other far more dangerous and mercenary rackets.'

'I see.' But I don't.

'I'm not a drug dealer, Lil.'

'What came in on the sixteenth, then?'

He sighs. 'Contraband. It didn't just come in on the sixteenth. It comes in all the time. I don't believe eighty-two percent of the price of anything should be tax. I feel like a modern day Robin Hood when I sell a packet of cigarettes or a bottle of whiskey for the right price.'

'But when we met you told me you were a gangster.'

He shook his head. 'You wanted to believe I was one. I just didn't disabuse you of the idea.'

'Luke told me you wanted to become a vet.'

'Yeah. A long time ago when I thought I could talk to animals and they talked back to me.'

I cover his hand with mine and tell him the story about the crows. The anger dissipates as I speak. His eyes become warm and full of some strong emotion. 'My grandmother still has all those shiny objects in a box,' I finish.

I see the glimmer of tears in his eyes.

'What is it?' I ask.

He shakes his head and for a long time he simply looks at me with an expression I have never seen before. I dare not name it. If it is what I think it is then it will reveal itself in time. I won't try to second guess it. It would be too frightening to do that in my delicate emotional state.

'Sometimes I don't know what to make of you, Lil. I'd love to meet your grandmother some day.'

'That's what she said,' I say with a smile.

He smiles back. 'Come on, let's get you home.'

'Sorry, I forgot to ask. Did you manage to solve your mother's problem?'

'Nope.'

'Oh?'

'Ask me why.'

I bite my lip. 'Why?'

'Because while praying she had a vision. She saw me with blood pouring out of my chest and you standing over me. You were the cause.'

I stare at him in shock. The idea is a terrifying, unimaginable vista. His words are like a monstrous tsunami wave rolling forward to envelop and swallow me whole. Foam and lies crash around me. In sheer panic I gasp a single breath of air. It rushes violently into my lungs. There is ice, too. In my heart.

'I don't want to hurt you, ever,' I whisper.

His eyes suddenly soften. 'I know,' he says quietly.

'I'm going to go into work tomorrow. I need to tell them that my cover is blown and that I really need to be taken off this case. In fact, I need to tell them that there is no case. Jake Eden is no kingpin drug dealer.'

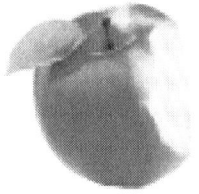

'Ah, my little lost lamb. Strayed into a den of
wolves, did ya?'

EIGHT

Lily

The next morning Jake kisses me tenderly on the forehead.

'Are you absolutely sure you don't want this done through a lawyer? All I have to do is pick up a phone and you'll never need to see any of them ever again.'

'I'm not afraid, Jake. I want to do this.'

'All right, but no matter what happens, never forget I'm here to support you,' he murmurs. His eyes are intense and full of some strong emotion.

'I think I kinda already know what's going to happen. I'm gonna get the book thrown at me,' I say softly.

'Call me when the meeting is over, OK?'

'OK.'

I dress carefully in a long black skirt, a striped white and gray shirt and a mannish gray jacket. I pull my hair back in a severe bun and stand in front of the mirror. And the mirror says, 'Slut in disguise.' I slick on some pale lipstick and I go to my meeting with DS Mills.

Sitting in the taxi I realize that I don't feel any emotional attachment to my job or to staying in the force. I have no fear of being disciplined, suspended, or even fired. I look at my hands and they are steady and lying relaxed on my handbag. The calmness stays while I go into the building, up the stairs, and down the familiar corridor to the double stable doors. I have a sudden memory of my first trip here. How nervous I'd been. Getting this job had seemed like the most important thing to me. I smiled to think of me then. I have changed.

I push open the stable doors and the usual gaggle of macho men are gathered about regaling each other with tales of their exploits. Robin is not around.

'How's it going, Strom?' one of the men shouts.

'Not bad,' I say, knowing that in less than an hour every one of them will have heard what I have done. The thing is, I don't care. Let them laugh. I glance at my watch. I am perfectly on time. I knock on DS Mills' door and he barks for me to come in.

I close the door behind me.

'Have a seat,' he invites.

'I gather Robin has told you my cover is blown,' I say, sitting down opposite him.

'Yes, you gather right.' He seems unwilling to say anything else. I realize he wants me to 'spill the beans'.

'I didn't tell him I was an undercover officer. He guessed—'

'How?'

'He said I was too clean and too innocent to be a runaway.'

He grunts.

'And Robin also probably told you that we got married.'

He nods. 'He didn't tell me why.'

'He said he married me because that way no one could force me to testify against him.'

'Right. That makes better sense. Are you in love with him?'

'Yes.'

'Is he in love with you?'

'I don't know. He hasn't said.'

'But he has strong feelings.'

I bite my lip. 'Yes. Yes, he has, but the thing is, Sir, I really think we have the wrong guy.'

'Why is that, then?' he drawls.

'Jake Eden is not a drug dealer. I've never once seen anybody take drugs in the club or seen anything that even looks like a drug deal going down. The only thing he seems to be doing is some harmless contraband.'

DS Mills' eyebrows fly upwards and I realize immediately that I shouldn't have used the word harmless. It has clearly revealed my loyalties.

'Smuggling is illegal and carries with it a criminal conviction and a prison sentence for those involved,' he says sarcastically.

'I thought we're going for the big criminals,' I say, hoping to lead him away from my mistake.

'Jake Eden *is* a big criminal.'

'He is not,' I cry passionately.

A look of amusement comes into his cold, ambitious eyes. 'On what are you basing your judgment?'

'He told me.' Oh, that came out wrong.

'And you believed him?' He shakes his head incredulously. 'What did you expect him to do? Tell you the truth when he knows you are an undercover cop?'

I look at him with frustrated eyes.

'I'm afraid, Strom, you have broken the undercover agent's cardinal rule.' His tone is surprisingly calm. 'You've allowed yourself to become emotionally involved with your target. And once your feelings are involved you are easy to manipulate.'

For a moment I don't speak. There is something else going on. I realize that he is toying with me. He is not angry that I fucked up the investigation by sleeping with the target. It occurs to me suddenly that he wanted me to. I was chosen purely for my looks. He hung me in front of Jake as if I was some kind of bait! Shocked, I watch him lean back into his chair, his face laced with a certain smugness.

'When you say harmless contraband, do you actually know what it is that he is bringing in?'

'I believe it's mainly cigarettes and alcohol,' I say cautiously.

He pins me with his eyes. 'Are you sure contraband is not a euphemism for cocaine, heroin and human trafficking?'

I stare at him filled with dread. He wants me to continue! It is not going to be as simple as I thought. *You are no longer impartial, your cover is blown, and you are taken off the case, Strom.* Why would Mills continue with an operation especially when the agent has fucked up so badly?

His calmness tells me that he must have known from the moment he chose me, an absolute amateur, that Jake would suss me out quickly, and with my cover blown, it would be the perfect opportunity to exploit both Jake and me. My blood runs cold. I study him carefully.

'I've seen the file, and other than the old stuff when he was working for that Schitt guy there is hardly anything there. What makes you so sure he is what you say he is?'

His eyes glitter dangerously. 'Instinct. When you do this job for long enough you develop strong feelers. Crystal Jake may have the cream of society fooled, but not me. I know his type. I know him.'

'What is it you want me to do?'

He smiles for the first time since I came into the room. 'I want you to go back to Jake Eden and pretend that you have been suspended pending an investigation into your behavior. And since you will be definitely living with him while the investigation is going on you will be thrown off the force. He has to feel so comfortable with...his new wife who is so deeply in love with him that she can never be compelled to testify against him that he loses his inclination to be guarded and starts boasting about what he is really bringing into this country. Rather than it being a setback, what has happened will make Crystal Jake far more accessible to us.'

Mills' smile suddenly breaks into laughter.

'What's so amusing?' I try not to show my irritation.

'The irony of it.'

'Irony?'

'Yes, isn't it ironic that the action he took to protect himself has actually made him more vulnerable?' He laughs again, but this time, I know, he is laughing at me.

I drop my head and stare at my handbag. It is black and it has a gold button and a gold buckle. I bought it cheap in a sale in John Lewis. I will need a new one soon. The edges are beginning to fray. His words are actually painful, cutting through every layer of my being like a well-sharpened knife. I am an amateur and he has played me easily. When he said, 'I know his type. I know him,' what he was saying was, Didn't I choose you? Didn't I know what would turn him on? Didn't I know you would play the role of slut perfectly?

I feel the blood bubbling in my veins with rage. Rage at being taken for a fool, rage at being used as a pawn for his ambitions, rage at the utter contempt that he has for me. He *knows* I'm in love with Jake and yet he is willing to sacrifice me to get what he wants. I stand suddenly and with such force that the chair skitters on its wheels across the small room and hits the opposite wall.

Mills gets up from his seat and walks without haste toward the chair. I turn and, with my hands gripping my handbag's strap so hard the knuckles show bone white, watch him pull the chair back to where I am standing. He looks me directly in the eyes.

'Sit down, Strom.' For a moment I hesitate. His voice is extraordinarily calm. Then I do as he commands and sit.

'I'm going to ignore what just happened, and put it down to the stress that comes with being undercover, particularly for a new operative.' He moves back around to his side of the desk and rests his palms on the surface of the desk before looming down over me.

'Do you still want to be in the police force, Strom?'

The answer takes me by surprise. It is a clear no. 'Yes, of course,' I say.

'Good. Bringing a criminal like Jake Eden to justice will ensure that you rise quickly up the metaphorical ladder of success and recognition. Do you understand?'

I nod.

'Very good. Now, do you feel you are able to carry out the plan I have laid out for you?'

I feel the beat of my heart high in my throat. 'Yes, Sir.'

'Excellent. From now on you will no longer make any contact with anyone other than me in this office. To all intents and purposes you are suspended. You will also have to vacate your company flat as soon as possible. We'll meet in the Bayswater safe house, and make contact with each other in exactly the same way Robin and you have established.' He opens his drawer and takes out an envelope. He puts it in front of me. 'The key is inside, along with my number and the address. Learn them by heart and destroy the information before you leave this office.' Wow! He had everything ready. How meticulously he has planned Jake's downfall.

'I want names, places, dates. Anything at all.' Mills' eyes are steely.

'Yes, Sir.'

'Any questions?'

'No, Sir,' I say, slitting open the envelope and staring at the phone number and the address on the paper. I commit them to memory and put the paper back on his desk. I take the key out of the envelope and put it into my handbag. Then I stand, even though he has not dismissed me.

A look of fury passes through his eyes. It is gone very quickly. 'I'll be waiting for a call from you.'

'Good day, Sir.' I walk to the door and when my hand is on the handle his words brush my skin like a cold hand.

'Do it for your brother.'

I turn around slowly.

He smiles. 'It wasn't on your file, but it is a matter of public record.'

I nod distantly, my thoughts well hidden.

Outside his door I see Robin leaning against a wall talking to someone, but I can see that he has been waiting for me to come out. I don't want to speak to him. I'm not allowed to, anyway. I wave. He raises his eyebrows as if to ask if I am OK. I show him the thumbs-up sign. He appears surprised, but I quickly walk out of the stable doors. I walk out of the offices and outside the sky is blue and the sun is shining. But I feel cold inside. I have just become a kind of double agent.

I could have walked out of Mills' office and been more than content to leave the force forever, but I know Mills won't stop in his mission to destroy Jake. His determination has become personal and obsessive. It is clear to me that, of the two men, Mills is far more dangerous and unscrupulous in his methods. Me walking away will only mean that I will no longer have any idea of what Mills is planning. I have to find a way to exonerate Jake. Call it sixth sense, or intuition, but something just doesn't make sense. I'll play his game until I get to the bottom of it.

I pass a street painter. He is chalking a large hole in the pavement with people falling in. It looks remarkably real. It seems a shame that talent like that should be so temporary.

I hail a cab to the company apartment in Vauxhall. I pack my things quickly. There is not much. Then I call another taxi, put the keys through the letterbox, and give the driver Jake's address.

As soon as I have put my stuff in the spare room in Jake's house, I text him.

Have been suspended from duty pending investigation.

The phone rings almost instantly. It is Jake. I have already decided that I will not tell him too much. Rule number one—always keep a little back for yourself. For later. For protection.

'What's going on, Lily?' he asks urgently.

His voice makes me feel a little guilty. I should have texted earlier, but I wanted to be clear in my head about what I was going to do.

'I told them that I had slept with you and married you. And that you had figured out that I was an undercover officer anyway. For my trouble I got suspended. Pending a full investigation, I could be dismissed from the police force.'

'Where are you now?'

'At home. I cleared out my stuff from the Vauxhall apartment and brought it here.'

'You should have called me earlier. I could have got someone to do it for you.'

'No, they wouldn't have known my stuff from the other girls'.'

'Are you all right?'

'I guess so.'

'Do you want me to come back?'

'No, absolutely not. There's nothing for you to do, anyway. We'll just end up having sex or something.'

He chuckles. 'I'll be there in five.'

'Honestly, Jake, I'm all right. I need a bit of time alone.'

'All right, we'll talk when I get back.'

'OK.'

'Lily...?'

'Yeah?'

'Never mind. I'll be home early. We'll talk then.'

'Bye.'

'See you soon.'

I put the phone down and think about the words we use with each other and the undercurrents beneath those cautious phrases. I desperately wanted to say I love you, but I bit it back. I wonder what he really wanted to say to me.

NINE

Lily

I go to see my mother.

Her voice bubbles up warmly toward me. 'Have you eaten?' she asks.

'Yes,' I say automatically.

'What time is it?'

'Eleven o'clock.'

'Come into the kitchen. I made a chocolate cake yesterday and iced it this morning. You might as well have some.'

I follow her into the kitchen. My mother has a large kitchen built for her by my dad, who is a bit of a DIY enthusiast. It is airy, clutter free and the exact opposite of Nan's kitchen. There is no kitchen god here. No incense. No sticky cakes, and no firecrackers during the Lunar New Year. She switches on the kettle and reaches for the tin where the tea bags are stored. I don't offer to help because I know she will refuse. She puts two mugs out next to the kettle.

'I've been so worried about you.' She twists the top off the tin and drops a tea bag in each mug. 'I don't think I quite like you being an undercover cop. I've read such horrible things.' She opens a drawer, takes out a knife then walks toward the cake stand where a beautifully iced cake is sitting under glass. 'What if someone offers you drugs? Are you supposed to take them?' She lifts the glass dome.

'Mum, I've left the force.'

Her hands still. She puts the glass dome on the counter, and turns around to stare at me, her face suddenly creased with concern and worry. 'Left the force? What happened?'

I sigh. 'It's a long story, Mum. I'll tell you another day.'

'Does this mean that you are now unemployed?'

I sigh. 'No, I have another job.'

'Doing what?'

'Admin work.'

'Does it pay well?'

'Better than being a police officer, that's for sure. Listen, Mum, forget my job for a minute, I wanted to tell you something more important.'

'What?' she asks almost suspiciously.

'I got married.'

'Oh! When?' she says looking shocked.

I show her the rings. She walks toward me and in a daze takes my hand. I realize then that my mother and I hardly touch. It's been so long since I have felt the texture of her skin.

'How did I not notice it? Did you not want Dad and me to be there then?' She sounds hurt and lost.

I bite my lip with remorse. I realize that I shouldn't have told her. Maybe I should have stayed silent, and if it all works out with Jake we should have just got married again.

'It was a spur of the moment thing. We were in Las Vegas. There was no family from either of us there.'

She lets go of my hand and frowns. 'You were in Las Vegas?'

'Yes, just for the weekend.'

'Dad's been saving up for a wedding for you,' she says softly.

'He can use the money to take you on a nice holiday,' I say, feeling like a total bitch. But what else can I tell her?

'Who is this man?'

'His name is Jake Eden.'

'Jake Eden,' she repeats softly. 'You've never spoken of him before.'

I nearly raise my eyebrows and say, When have I ever spoken to you or Dad about a man? But I catch myself in time and say, 'It was a bit of a whirlwind thing.'

She looks deep into my eyes. 'I'm glad you're happy.'

'I am,' I tell her firmly.

She smiles. 'What does he do?'

I tell her what will satisfy her. 'He's a businessman.'

'Good,' she says approvingly. 'Do you have a photograph?'

'No, I'll bring him over next week.'

'That'll be nice. Dad will want to meet him.' She turns away from me and cuts two slices of cake.

Poor Mum. Her world seems so small, so pointless. For years Dad and I have protected her from all bad news. So now she lives her life baking and cleaning and watching soaps. Sometimes Dad and I intrude into her life and she reacts with surprise. And I realize it from her that I have learned to be so distant with the ones I love.

We eat her cake—it is delicious—and drink tea together.

Once she puts her fork down and asks again, 'Are you happy, Lily?'

I look her in the eye. 'Yes, Mother. I am.'

She smiles and I smile back and for a few seconds it feels as if the sun is shining in my mother's small world.

'That's good,' she says. 'That's very good.'

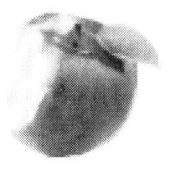

Jake

We go to Lily's parents' home for dinner. They live in a Victorian three bedroom semi in Hampstead. The décor is pure Scandinavian: white walls, cool blue rugs and brown leather furniture. But an air of immutable sadness permeates it. Here there are unhealed and grievous wounds. Even Lily seems sadder and smaller. She smiles at me uncertainly and it makes me want to hold and reassure her, but I don't. I realize that it is not the done thing in the Strom household. Here everybody is an island unto themselves.

Her father is white-haired, tall, thin, and appears much older than his years, and her mother is small, fragile, and charming. To my surprise she cooks and serves up a superb five-course meal. There is Gravadlax of salmon, pea velouté, an apple and mint sorbet between courses, noisettes of lamb and perfectly cooked vegetables. She finishes with poached oranges and pots of crème brûlée to rival the ones you'd find in the best five star restaurants. Afterwards, we nibble on excellent chocolate truffles.

'Homemade,' Lily's father proudly informs.

I compliment her mother, again.

She smiles modestly.

The family dynamics are interesting. The mother in all her fragility utterly controls her family. Both husband and daughter treat her as if she is fashioned out of eggshell and defer to her in all things.

In the car, Lily doesn't ask me what I think of her parents and I don't offer any opinion. The evening is a success on the surface, but I think I both terrified and fascinated them, in the way a colorful but poisonous reptile might. As for me they are not really my kind of people, they are too straight and proper—not an unpaid parking ticket between them no doubt. Their marriage reminds me of the surface of a pond, stale and passionless. Still, I like them well enough.

In all their careful goodness they made my Lily.

TEN

Lily

After I paint my lips carmine, I step into a long, backless black dress that ties at the nape of my neck. One little tug and I'll be standing in a scrap of lace held together by a bit of string. Carefully I pin a small black brooch on the tie, then step into a pair of black shoes with gold high heels. My toenails, painted gold, poke through. I stand in front of the mirror and look at myself curiously. I have never worn black. Nan's superstitions have colored my thoughts.

'Bad luck color. For funerals only,' she always said.

But Jake bought this dress for me, and now that I see myself in it I realize that I really like black. I think it makes me look long and sophisticated. I touch my meticulously constructed hairdo and wonder what the night will bring. Tonight is the big re-launch party for Eden. Everyone will be there. It is an event.

As I finish fixing a pair of gold hoops in my ears, Jake appears in the doorway. I turn around to look at him and my breath catches. I have never seen him look so dashing. He is wearing a snow white dress shirt, a black silk tie, a beautifully cut black suit and black shoes. There is a red carnation pinned to his lapel. Nothing adds panache to a man's appearance like the confidence embodied in wearing a boutonnière, that symbol of fragile life and beauty caught in a single bloom. I already know that he will be the only man in the entire club wearing a flower on his left breast. The only man swimming against the current. And I love him for it.

He comes forward and stands next to me.

'We match,' I say to our reflections.

'That we do, but you are more beautiful by far,' he compliments suavely.

I smile, wordless, swept up by his beauty, by my good fortune, by the intensity of my feelings.

As he watches I tilt my head back, elongate my neck amorously, and with a single finger, dab perfume behind my ears and at the base of my throat.

In the mirror I see him turn toward me. His hands go toward my earrings. 'Not these for tonight,' Jake whispers, as he gently removes them. From his pocket he brings out two strands of blue gems. Carefully, he hangs them from my ears. My mouth drops open in amazement. They are indescribably gorgeous. I turn my head slightly and the ropes of blue swing into my neck.

'Oh, Jake. They are beautiful,' I gasp.

 85

But he is not finished. From his other pocket he takes another handful of blue gems, and moving to the back of me, places them around my throat. The stones glitter against my skin, like blue stars. Their color is so close to the shade of my eyes that I gaze at them in astonishment. *How did he find these stones?* My eyes meet his, startled, wondering, and awestruck. He smiles and turns me around to face him.

'I was right. They are perfect,' he murmurs, and bending his head kisses the hollow between my breasts where the plunging neckline ends. He watches riveted as through the material my nipples harden. He runs his palms over them and I make a small sound of submission.

His eyes register approval. 'I can't wait to get you home tonight.' There is a softness and depth to his voice.

In the darkened confines of the car I feel Jake's hand take mine.

'Your hands are cold,' he says. 'You're not nervous, are you?'

'A bit.'

He squeezes my hand. 'Don't be. I'll be at your side the whole time.'

I smile gratefully at him.

'You do know you will be the most beautiful woman in there.'

'You haven't even seen all the women yet.'

'I don't need to. You are the most beautiful woman to me.'

As we approach the queue of people waiting to get in I feel a little apprehensive, but also a heady sense of excitement. The new Eden's marbled and gilt splendor seems almost garish to my heightened senses. I feel so buoyed up I am almost light-headed. My feet seem to scarcely touch the ground and my stomach feels empty. I suppose it could be because I haven't eaten for hours. I daren't eat, not with this dress. Perhaps I am also anxious that I may not fit in. The shadow of his mother's disapproval looms. I know she will be here. Will she undermine me?

Red ropes are lifted and we are ushered in.

We go past the plum velvet loveseat in the foyer toward the enormous central vase filled with magnolia blossoms. Struck by two spotlights the blooms seem almost brighter than the lamps.

The music grows louder and my heartbeat quickens.

We enter the club and the whole of fashionable London seems to be there. All the dancers are in their best, and beautiful people are everywhere. It must be true that beautiful models, male and female, have been flown in from all over the world to pretty up the place. Under the chandeliers the supremely rich are casually amused and the air is charged with their intriguingly corrupt whiff. Laughter ebbs and flows like the tide.

The Mayor of London is present; movie star hair, sharp as knives, and as usual pretending to be a good-natured buffoon.

Jake takes me to the table where his mother is sitting. Her eyes meet mine and her back straightens. She drops her eyes to a large bowl of floating orchids set in the middle of the table.

'Ma,' he greets, and bends to kiss her. In the candlelight the pearls around her neck glimmer milkily. She appears softened and yet hostile.

'Hello, Mrs. Eden,' I greet politely.

She nods distantly. I can't blame her. I might be even more ferocious if I thought someone was threatening my son. I remember being in school and aggressively fighting Luke's battles for him.

'Lily, meet my sister, Layla,' Jake says.

I turn to meet a stunning creature in a deep red silk dress standing next to us. She is tall, very tall—she might even be five ten or eleven—and is everything I have always thought of as beautiful. Her hair is the color of bitter chocolate and cascades down her back in rich and lustrous waves. Her eyes are as green as Jake's, but there appears to be either gray or

 88

blue in them, too. Her nose is straight and narrow, and her mouth is large and expressive. She grins, vibrantly alive and fiery. She is only nineteen and Jake tells me she has been studying fashion in Paris.

'Layla, Lily.'

Layla claps her hands with delight. 'Oh, Jake. She's a doll.'

I visualize the expression on my mother-in-law's face, extract the disapproval and count the hatred.

Jake looks down at me, indulgent, almost like a proud parent. 'Yes, she is a bit of a doll, isn't she?'

Heat warms up my throat and cheeks.

But in seconds the dynamics of the situation change.

'Who the fuck invited him?' Layla says angrily. The change in her is dramatic to say the least. There are twin spots of color in her cheeks.

'I did,' Jake says smoothly.

I turn my eyes in the direction Layla is looking in and see Billy Joe Pilkington approaching us. He is impossible to miss. He is large and menacing. Everything about him screams *beware of me, I'm lethal.* He is the kind of man I would cross the road to avoid. When he was bloodied and lying beside Jake, the menace had not been so apparent. Now it powers out of him in waves. He is dressed in a navy suit, but he is not wearing a tie, and his shirt is open low enough to see the beginnings of his tattoos. His eyes are dark—either dead fire or black ice. A place to trip up and fall badly.

He stops by Jake's mother first. 'Good health to you, Mrs. Eden,' he says.

Mara smiles. 'God and Mary to you. How is your mother?'

'She's made dying her life's work,' he says with a straight face.

Jake's mother hides a smile. 'May God grant her many years.'

'And me earplugs,' he says with a wink, and turns his attention toward our group of three.

'Hello, Layla,' he greets civilly.

'You have a nerve coming here!' she says rudely. Her whole body has become strangely stiff and hostile. She looks at him with great disdain.

'Layla,' her mother gasps, shocked.

'Apologize, Layla,' Jake says with a scowl.

'Why should I?' Layla retorts.

But BJ grins at her. It has an odd effect on his face. It does not soften it, but makes it even more dangerous. 'Layla,' he says softly. 'Look at you, all grown up and still not a shred of manners in sight.'

'See?' Layla turns to her mother. 'He's not being exactly friendly to me, is he?'

They stare at each other for a few seconds. The aggressive sexual tension between them is impossible to miss and makes me wonder which of them is actually resisting it.

'Maybe you'll save a dance for me later?' he says, a dimple forming in his chin. Shit. The guy is actually attractive.

'Hell will freeze over first,' she declares dramatically and flounces off.

BJ laughs, his eyes chasing her into the crowd.

'Sorry about that,' Jake says.

'No, don't apologize for her. She's got spirit. I like that in women and horses.'

Jake laughs. 'Let's call for a drink.'

A waitress materializes and while we are placing our orders another comes around with a tray of little round bruschetta with glistening swordfish carpaccio. The drinks arrive. BJ raises his pint glass of Guinness in a toast.

'Here's to cheating, stealing, fighting, and drinking.'

'May you be in heaven half an hour before the devil knows you're dead,' Jake replies.

We clink glasses. We drink. As ice-cold champagne slides down my throat I see Melanie waving at me. I haven't seen her since Jake came and took me and all my stuff from the flat I shared with her. I know she can't come over to our section so I excuse myself. 'I'm just going to say hello to a friend.' I glance at Jake and mouth, 'Be back soon.'

I weave my way over to her and she grins at me and we exchange kisses that are almost sisterly. She is dressed in a white gown of ravishing simplicity. It flows down her body like liquid. Her lips are ruby and her lashes are as long as an ostrich's.

'Girl, you sure showed us how to do it,' she shouts above the music and the din of the party.

I look back at Jake—he is watching me. I wave and laugh out loud. I know that for most of the dancers the holy grail is finding a fat purse and marrying it as quickly as possible. They know they can't dance after a certain age so the race is on as soon as they start out. Each one will say the same thing: They are here for a short spell.

Melanie is different, though. She is saving up to take the money to Barbados where she plans to buy a beach bar. The last time we talked she figured she would only have to work for another six months.

'Is that adoring admiration I just saw?' she teases.

I flush. 'Maybe.'

'Has he got a big dick?' she asks cheekily.

'Yes,' I admit and we giggle wickedly. I miss her blunt and honest ways.

'Wow, I love these,' she says, touching the blue stones.

'Me too,' I agree happily.

'Listen, I have to go because I'm performing now, but let's catch up soon.'

'All right. How about Friday?'

'Nails and then lunch?'

'OK, I'll call you.'

As I watch her walk away I notice the man who had come to collect BJ after the fight, the man who had shown for a split second that he recognized me.

I start walking toward him.

Our eyes meet, but he lets his slide away, pretending not to see me making my way toward him, tries to disappear through the crowd in the direction of the men's toilet. I let him escape. A few minutes later he comes out of the toilet and looks around him. He does not see me behind the pillar and is startled when I touch his sleeve.

He whirls around.

'Hi, remember me?' I say brightly.

He frowns as if trying to place me. 'Oh yeah, from the fight, right?'

'No, you know me from before, don't you?'

His frown deepens. He is a very good actor.

'No, I had never seen you before that day. You must have me mixed up with someone else.' He smiles, but his eyes are shifty, oh so fucking shifty.

'My mistake,' I say softly, but now I know for certain. He is lying. My eyes glance away from him and fall on BJ across the room. One of the South American dancers has wound herself around him, but he is staring at us. Even from a distance I can see how hard and dangerous his eyes are.

BJ's man opens his mouth to say something else, but is interrupted by Jake's voice. He has come up behind me and curved his hand

around my waist. 'Everything OK?' he asks icily. There is tension and warning in the words.

I look up at him. His eyes are dark and watchful.

'Everything's just fine.'

'Hello, Mr. Eden,' the liar says uncomfortably.

'Have a good evening, Tommy,' Jake says curtly, and turning me away leads me back to our table.

'The entertainment is about to start,' he says. Without BJ, Layla looks quiet and subdued. The nightclub becomes dark. Searching spotlights begin to race around the room.

From the darkened ceiling come cages with flaxen-haired nymphs who look like trapped birds inside. The music, a jarring discordant piece of hammering pianos and choppy chords, starts, and the nymphs hang out of their cages, and slowly spiral down on colored lengths of cloth. They land on the stage and form a provocative tableau of glittering costumes and long, stockinged legs. The music changes abruptly.

Something inventive and experimental. My ears start to ring with it.

It is a good evening and I have had more alcohol than I should have. When we step over the threshold of our home, Jake lets go of me and I sway slightly.

'Is it today or tomorrow?' I ask, pretending to consider the matter seriously.

He glances at his watch. 'It's today and tomorrow,' he says very, very gravely. He could be laughing at me, but I don't care. He won't be laughing for very long.

'In that case...' I tug the knot. Just before we left the club I visited the Ladies and took off the little brooch that held the knot. Now it gives way and the entire dress falls around my ankles.

He touches my breasts with the tips of his fingers. As soon as he touches them I feel his excitement like a spark of electricity and rear back.

'What's that?' I ask startled.

'That's amazement,' he tells me solemnly.

'That makes two of us.' I say flirtatiously.

'Guess what?' His eyes are cheeky.

'What?' I'm all wide-eyed and ready.

'I stole some stuff from our room in Vegas.'

'Oh yeah? What?'

'Come with me, Mrs. Eden, and I'll show you.'

Handcuffs. Oh! Handcuffs. They most certainly did not teach me everything there is to know about them at the police academy.

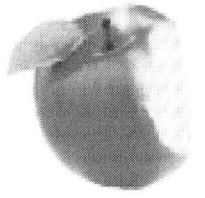

'What do I love more than my wife?
Nothing.'

—Jake Eden

ELEVEN

Lily

I wake in the early hours of the morning with a dream still vividly imprinted on my mind. It is an odd dream. In it I am a child and I have woken up and found Luke gone from his bed. Unafraid, I get out of bed and go down the stairs. The house is quiet so I begin to call out for him. There is no sense of foreboding. As I move to the living room I see there is a plate of cookies and a glass of milk on the floor. And then I wake up.

I lay in the dark thinking about my weird dream; it ushers in a memory of when I was six years old and Luke five. It was Christmas morning and the moment I'd opened my excited eyes the first thought in my head was the presents that Santa brought us during the night. He always left two presents at the bottom of our beds to open first thing in the morning. I turned my head to see if Luke was awake yet, and found that he was not even in bed. Surprised, because we always woke each other up and opened our presents together, I sat up and listened. The house was very quiet.

I knew he couldn't have gone to the bathroom anyway, because he'd rather pee in bed than wait to open his presents. I scrambled out of bed and ran to the bedroom window that faced a field overlooking the woods at the rear of our house.

I opened the curtains and there were almost blizzard conditions outside. Through driving snow I could make out Luke's bright yellow jacket. He was squatting in the middle of the white field building something from the snow, oblivious to the freezing cold. He'd slipped out of our bedroom, down the stairs and gone outside through the back door, without even Mum or Dad hearing him.

Shrugging into my pink jacket I hurried downstairs as quietly as I could. I knew my parents would be mad with Luke and I was so excited about Christmas Day I didn't want anything to spoil it. I opened the back door and felt the sudden bite of cold. I didn't dare shout so I went quite close before I called out to him.

'What are you doing, Luke?'

He stopped building what looked like three steps of a snow staircase and squinted at me through the flurries of white flakes. His little cheeks were tinged with red and blue.

'If Mum and Dad see you they're going to go mad on Christmas,' I warned.

He reached for a toy tractor half covered with snow.

'I don't want Santa's present.'

'Why?' I asked perplexed. He had specifically asked for this toy. Stood in Toys"R"Us and pointed it out to Dad as the thing that Santa should bring him.

'I've changed my mind,' he said with his bottom lip pushed out stubbornly. 'I want to go to Santa and get an exchange, so I'm making a ladder to climb to the North Pole.'

'What do you want to exchange your present for?' I asked curiously.

'I want Santa to make mummy better.'

How strange that that memory is intact and yet has been hidden from me all these years. Remembering those words from his tiny mouth breaks my heart, and tears rush uncontrollably forward. I begin to cry for my baby brother.

Very quietly, I edge to the side of the bed and slip out. Going into the bathroom I climb into the bath and hug my knees to my body as the tears flow. I remember how my dad found us both building the staircase and managed to convince Luke that we could write to Santa. Santa preferred that, anyway.

That is the thing I'll always remember and miss about Luke, his kind heart and beautiful innocence. He was a gentle dreamer and life should have treated him with care and love, but it didn't.

'Oh, Luke,' I whisper.

I hear a small sound at the door, the whisper of clothes against wood. I look up and Jake is standing there looking at me.

'What are you doing?' he asks me. His eyes are full of concern.

'I want to tell you about my brother,' I tell him.

'OK,' he says and climbs into the bath and sits facing me, his toes nearly touching mine.

'He was a heroin addict and he died from an overdose.' My voice catches at that. I have never admitted that to anyone before. 'I found his body.'

Something flashes in his eyes, but he does not say anything or attempt to hold me.

'It was truly awful. It destroyed me. I became a little mad after that.' I laugh, a rasping, desperate sound. He says nothing. Simply looks at me. I clear my throat and I tell him about the spoon, the rubber tube. The needle still embedded in his bloated arm. Then I tell him about my descent.

'I was barely living. I survived on a mixture of rage and the need for revenge. I was so broken I even tried to kill myself.'

I peer into his eyes, looking for condemnation of my weakness, or pity, but there is nothing, only direct and tenacious focus. At that moment I know I can tell him anything and he will still be there for me. His regard is unshakeable.

I come clean. 'Everything I told you about my parents so far has been lies, part of my cover story. My dad, he's not an alcoholic or a wife beater. He's a good man, a doctor. He put me on anti-psychotic drugs.'

Then I pour out the visit to the pathologist and how it made me so angry with the people who had sold the tainted drugs to Luke that I decided to become a police officer. I tell him about how I joined the secretive undercover outfit called SO10. I tell him about the crack den and how the terrible, terrible smell of it still haunts me. And how I realized very quickly that I didn't want to go after the small dealers, but the huge drug barons, and how the assignment to trap Crystal Jake had dropped into my lap.

'So you went undercover. To catch the big bad guys?' he asks.

I nod.

'If you come upon a case where a wealthy heiress has died under suspicious circumstances and you are the investigating officer, what is the first line of investigation that you would naturally take?'

I frown. 'I'd follow the money.'

'So if you want to catch the big drug barons, why are you not following the money?'

For a second I am confused. 'I'm a foot soldier. It is not my job to do that. My superiors decide the avenues of investigation and I carry out their commands.'

'Has it ever occurred to you to wonder why no one at the highest levels of this "drug war" is doing that?'

I frown again, thrown by the turn the conversation has taken. 'What are you saying?'

'I'm saying that you, your little secretive undercover unit, and all the other departments that are supposed to be fighting the drugs war are all being manipulated. Drug barons are worth billions. They have to wash their money somewhere. That somewhere is some of the biggest banks in the world. Why are they sending you out to trap me when the most obvious thing would be to punish the banks that hide the money, to freeze the billions that the drug cartels own, and to stop the drugs at the source?'

I stare at him. Feeling stupid. It is an issue that I care about very deeply and yet I have accepted the most shallow of explanations about it.

'The most developed form of puppetry in the world is the traditional Japanese puppet theater called Bunraku. The Japanese are very proud of it because it is considered a very highly skilled art form. And it is rather special because unlike other puppet shows the manipulators of the Bunraku puppets appear openly, in full view of the audience. However, the audience pretends not to be able to see them because the puppet masters are cloaked in black robes and sometimes black hoods.

'The war on drugs is the same. The real manipulators of the puppets are not invisible, but we pretend we can't see them. The system has trained us to see only the small-time criminals, the powerless puppets. So they train people like you to go after small fry and to be happy you have shut down a drug den knowing full well that as long as supply is safe another den will pop up even before the arresting officers have written their reports.'

He pauses.

'But as far as I am concerned I'm not even that small-time drug dealer, Lily. You have to believe me.'

'So why do they want you?'

'You tell me.'

I press my fingertips against my temples. 'I have seen the file on you.'

'I haven't touched drugs since I was nineteen years old. Whatever you saw in that file is not me. You see, I've been in a crack den a few times. I've seen clawing addiction first-hand. That intolerable smell you talk about, that's feces, the ammonia of stale urine, sweat, and layers of accumulated dirt. And those blankets that they put up to cover every little gap of light that would otherwise come through? They do that because of their paranoia. They have the unshakable impression that people are watching them.'

'Were you a crack addict?' I whisper in shock.

He smiles. 'No, but I know because I was once that slightly bigger fish drug dealer that all those little drug dealers went to, to get their stock from. I went to a crack house so I could see the bottom of my chain. It made me so sick I started a charity to help them. I don't have a lot of time so I don't do as much as I should, but if you want to help them you can take over. We both know you are bored sick of your job.'

'How did you know I was bored?'

He flattens his mouth. 'Lily, that job was designed to bore the shit out of you.'

'What?'

'Of course. What, did you think I was going to put you into some position where you could get any kind of information that could be twisted and used against me?'

'Right. What does your charity do?'

'We send the addicts to South America to be purged out with ayahuasca assisted treatments. It may seem off the wall but it has been shockingly effective and the reoffend rate is better than anything else I have seen.'

'Doesn't that have a psychedelic chemical, DMT, a Schedule 1 controlled substance?'

'Ayahuasca is a psychoactive brew of vine and plants that has been used in traditional medicine and shaman practices for centuries in the Amazon region. It is perfectly legal in South America.'

'Right,' I say carefully, since I know nothing about this stuff, but my first thought is that if it works that well, why isn't it on mainstream media?

'International research suggests that when administered in therapeutic settings, ayahuasca can reduce problematic substance use by helping promote personal or spiritual insights and self-knowledge. That's the spiel we give our detractors. This is my experience of it.

It's fucking brilliant. These kids go there like walking corpses, they projectile vomit, shit like crazy, experience strong audio and visual hallucinations, and come out a few weeks later healed and whole. It is a form of psychic detoxification where they discover the root cause—unpleasant memories, fears, anxieties—of their addictive and harmful behavior. Sometimes that sense of deficient emptiness and inchoate distress that they have felt all their life is gone. It gives them their first taste of victory after being constantly defeated by life. They come to the understanding that they are already the perfect human beings they were born as.'

I experience a stab of pain. Poor Luke. It's too late for him.

'Have you tried it?'

'Of course. I wasn't about to let the kids go through something I wasn't going to try first.'

'What was it like?'

He smiles. 'Ayahuasca shows you the baggage you have carried all your life. You see clearly that all that pain is not part of you. You can put it down. I cried tears of pure joy when I took it. If you want I'll take you one day.'

I look into his eyes and I know instantly that I would like to do that. I'd like to heal, too. I'd like to put my baggage down and live like everybody else.

'Why don't you go around to the center tomorrow and see how you feel about it?'

'I will.' I pause for a second. There is something more important for me to tackle before I get involved in his charity. 'Do you have enemies, Jake?'

'Many.'

'Someone is out for you. Someone is giving untrue information about you.'

'And you think it is Tommy?'

I look up at him, surprised by how quickly he has surmised the situation. 'Yes.'

'Why?'

'Because when I came to pick you up at the barn after the fight he looked at me as if he knew me, but I have never seen him before in my life.'

'And BJ? You think he's involved too?'

'If you were out, he could move in and claim your territory, right?'

He nods slowly. I open my mouth to say something else, but he puts a finger against my lips. 'Don't say anything for a while.'

We sit staring at each other, trying to insert some normality into the scene we find ourselves playing.

Finally, he says, 'Don't tell anyone what you just told me.'

I nod.

'Promise me, Lily. You are making some very dangerous accusations. These people are lethal. You don't know the way they think. The question of honor is not taken lightly in our community. You have to promise to stay out of this. You've told me and you must trust me to sort it out, OK?'

'OK, I promise,' and that should have been the perfect time to tell him that I am still an undercover agent—not trying to trap him, but trying to help him. But I don't because I know he will try to stop me and I don't want to be stopped. I want to get to the bottom of the truth. I have been led by the nose too long.

Later I will regret my silence.

TWELVE

Lily

'**I** am bored with all the restaurants I know. Take me somewhere authentic, but Chinese obviously,' Melanie says after we do our nails.

The only restaurant that immediately comes to mind is the one that Robin once took me to. Even though the service was just shy of surly, the food was surprisingly good. We take a taxi to Soho and go into the restaurant. Like most Chinese restaurants the air conditioning is turned up too high. We are met at the till by an unsmiling waitress and briskly shown to our seats. A laminated, slightly sticky menu is thrust into our hands.

'You want drink?' she asks while noisily clearing away the extra table settings.

We order Chinese tea.

Melanie raises her eyebrows. 'Already I am impressed,' she says sarcastically.

'We Chinese, we tend to be a bit abrupt, but don't worry—the speed and taste of our food will make up for it,' I say in a heavily accented voice.

Melanie laughs but true to form the food arrives with impressive speed. The crispy Peking duck is so delicious Melanie eats more than I have ever seen her eat. Afterwards the egg fried rice, sea bass steamed with ginger and onions, cashew nut prawns, and a mixed vegetable dish arrive piping hot and go down quickly, too. We are nearly finished with our meal when Melanie suddenly chuckles quietly.

'What?' I ask her.

'This is what I love about dancing. You meet all kinds of people without their masks. Don't look now but the guy that has just come in used to come into Miss Moneypenny.'

I know that name. It is another gentlemen's club and if I am not mistaken it belongs to the Pilkingtons.

'Oh yeah?' I say casually. 'What's so special about him?'

'Well. He's arrived here with a policeman and they look really chummy so it's obvious he must be some kind of undercover cop too, but you should have seen him at the club. He has a taste for cruelty. He went for the dancers who were turning tricks on the sly. Once he took a girl home, and she never turned up for work the next day. We never saw her again while I was there. There was something fishy going on too. All the girls were talking about it. We all knew it was not right.'

My eyes widen with shock. 'What do you mean?'

'She was Romanian. No family. No relatives. Just disappeared. One moment she says, "Bye, see you tomorrow," and next minute she's gone without a trace. Management should have called the police. He was the last one to see her. But nothing happened. And now I know why. He *is* the police. Another time he beat a girl real bad. I heard that *she* was asked to leave! I didn't stay after that. Bad vibes, man.'

I feel a ripple of disgust go through me. There is a dirty cop behind me. 'Who runs that club?'

'You were talking to him yesterday. That slime ball, Tommy.'

I sit frozen. 'Right,' I say slowly. 'Can he see us, Melanie?'

'OK, he's looking at the menu. Quick, turn around and look now. He's the one in trendy yellow designer gear.'

I glance around as casually as I can and my limbs turn to water. I turn back quickly and look at her in shock. 'Are you sure, Melanie?'

'Of course I'm sure. I could never forget that bastard. All the girls were scared of him. It was as if he was the boss.'

'Does he know you?'

'I wouldn't have thought so. I'm not his flavor. He likes Eastern European girls, blondes.'

Her eyes narrow. 'You look like you've seen a ghost. Do you know him?'

I meet her gaze with a frown. 'Yes, I do, but I can't explain just yet.' I take a deep breath.

'Bejesus. You're mixed up with him.'

'Not in the way you think. Look, do you mind if we slip out through the back way? I don't want him to see me.'

She shrugs. 'OK.'

I call for the bill. While my credit card is being processed by the machine I look up at our unsmiling waitress. 'My ex-boyfriend has just turned up and it could be trouble for me, can I please leave by the back way?'

'Cannot. Regulations,' she says shortly.

I take a ten pound note out of my purse and put it into the tray. Her eyes slide down to it.

'I show you the way.'

At a dirty black door she turns to me. 'You come again,' she says with a smile and shuts the door in our faces.

'Come on, Mel,' I say pulling her away. As we hurry away my mind is whirling like crazy. The truth is I am actually frightened. I have the sensation that the ground I thought I was standing so securely upon has turned into quicksand that is sucking me up. Two streets away we hail a cab and I say goodbye to Melanie.

You know what kind of people become undercover officers? People who want to hide under a different skin, unhappy people, people with low self-esteem. On one hand I hate the people that I am supposed to be trapping; in another sense I become them and secretly envy them and their glamorous lifestyles.

I can hardly bring myself to believe that the man Melanie is talking about is Robin. That... That Robin is a bent cop.

Instead of getting another cab for myself I walk aimlessly along the street. I need to think. I know I need to arrange a meeting with Mills in the safe house, but I also know that whistleblowers in the force are not lauded and promoted but disappeared. Anyone who raises issues and problems becomes the problem. And it is doubly dangerous to be the problem of such an ambitious man as Mills. He wants Jake's head on a platter, not Robin's. So I need to protect myself.

I look at my watch. Jake isn't expecting me for a while yet. By leaving the restaurant via the back entrance we would have lost the tail Jake has on me. I disappear into the Tube and get out at Green Park. I exit and hailing a cab ask him to take me to Lea Bridge Road.

Ten minutes after I walk into Lorraine Electronic Surveillance I leave with their smallest audio recorder, a nifty device no bigger than a USB stick, but one that is powerful enough to clearly pick up sound at up to twenty-five feet. It also has a twelve hour record time and is sound activated, so will only begin recording when it hears something.

Then I call the number Mills gave me. To my surprise it is not a telephone operator who will pass on the message but Mills who answers. Our conversation is brief and to the point.

Tomorrow at noon.

Then I catch a cab back to Jake's home. Before Jake comes home that evening I book a rental car and have them park it in a car park that I specify. I pay for a courier to pick up the keys and drop it off to me inside the hour.

Then I sit down and plan my meeting with Mills. When Jake comes home he finds me cooking, a bottle of wine open, me on my second glass, the music so loud I don't hear him come in.

He leans against the doorway watching me.

I grin and point to his glass of whiskey. He picks it up and comes toward me. 'I didn't know we were having a party.'

'I have an Irish joke for you.'

He groans.

'No, no, it's really good.'

'Go on.'

'There's an Englishman, a Scotsman and an Irishman all talking about their teenage daughters. The Englishman says, "I was cleaning my daughter's room the other day and I found a packet of cigarettes. I was really shocked as I didn't even know she smoked."

'The Scotsman says, "That's nothing. I was cleaning my daughter's room the other day when I came across a half full bottle of vodka. I was really shocked as I didn't even know she drank."

'With that the Irishman says, "Both of you have got nothing to worry about. I was cleaning my daughter's room the other day when I found a packet of condoms. I was really shocked. I didn't even know she had a cock."'

Jake laughs and so do I.

That sets the tone for the evening. It is irreverent. We eat with our fingers and laugh a lot. I totally forget about Mills and what I have to do the next day.

Afterwards, Jake makes me wear a pair of my shoes from my dancing days and do a strip tease for him. Tipsy and laughing I start undressing. It is only a game. It is to put the night to bed.

But when I look into his darkened eyes, my mouth makes a purring sound and my sex swells, hot, wet and aching.

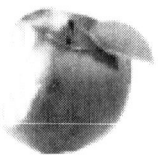

Jake

She seems different tonight, her face is flushed, her lips parted. Sweat dampens her naked skin. She is wild for it, in that desperate way that people have on the last day of their holiday. She grinds her bare ass against my erection and I groan and catch her by the waist, holding her tightly. She wriggles away. I let her go. She comes back like a carefree butterfly.

I watch her push the globes of creamy flesh close to my face and shimmy hard so all her flesh quivers and shakes. That heady, sexy as hell scent of her fills my nostrils and I feel myself losing control. My breathing becomes shallow, my heart races. Your time running around naked and free is nearly over, my love. She turns around to face me, her legs apart. Her folds are swollen and protrude invitingly out of her sex lips.

'Undress,' she orders, in a deep silky voice, utterly unaware of how improbable she sounds giving orders when her bits are protruding or how little time is left for her to play the tease. She's everything I've ever wanted.

My eyes never leaving hers, I tug off my clothes in double quick time. She spins around in a deft lap-dancer move and, pushing me down on the sofa, she moves upwards, and with her thighs wide open she begins to lower her sticky sex into my mouth. I watch it come down, the puffy lips oozing and glistening with raw sexual need, her hole gaping and begging to be filled.

Like a hungry man I swoop upwards to meet it on its way down to me. With her hands flat on either side of my hips she leans forward and slips her warm, open mouth over my engorged dick. The glaze of sweat makes her nipples slide against my body.

I hear the sound of her heart beating faster as her breath rasps with excitement. I lick and suck and fuck her with my tongue until she comes with a force that shakes her to her very core.

I spread her legs wide and look at her. Her gorgeous hair is tangled and spread across the sofa. Slowly I let my eyes travel down to her sex, open and ready for me, and I feel that wild, relentlessly primitive urge to possess and brand her. To mark her as mine. If I was in one of those tribal societies where they ink their women to mark them as their property I'd be right there inking her whole body so there is no mistaking what is mine.

Putting my hands on either side of her I mount her. Her mouth opens into a slack O. It gives me immense pleasure to know that the thick, mushroomed head of my cock is stretching her to unbearableness. She locks her legs desperately around my hips to keep me there. Just the idea of her underneath me, helplessly swallowing my cock into her body, excites me and I pound her hard until I explode inside her, my cock pushing so deep into her that her body buckles and shudders.

For a few seconds I stay inside her while she milks the cream of my body with her own. And during that time I sense her as if she is a part of my body, her heartbeat, the flow of blood inside her veins, the increased heat rising off her skin, and the lift and fall of her chest. The sensation is unfamiliar, but strangely beautiful. For a long time I watch the moonlight come in through the window and throw its blue light on her cheek. I want to protect her from anything and everything that could possibly hurt her.

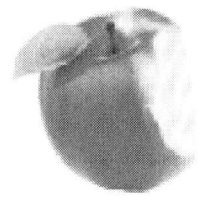

How foolish I was to think
That I could catch a butterfly?
　　　—*Butterflies*, Shiv Kumar Batalvi

THIRTEEN

Lily

At twelve I take a cab and direct it to an Indian restaurant in Notting Hill. I go into the restaurant, slip the waiter a twenty pound note, and he gladly escorts me out through the back door. I walk quickly along the back street, take a left and walk up the road to the NCP car park. Inside, I keep pressing the key remote in my hand until a car lights up and clicks open.

I get in and drive to the safe house, where I find a parking space, pay the parking charge and get out, locking the car. It is a small building of six flats in a quiet street. At lunchtime hardly anyone is around. I access the apartment block through the street entrance and climb briskly to the second floor. My heart is thudding hard, but I am not in a panic. I know I haven't done anything wrong. I think I am more bemused than anything else.

I check the concealment of my recording device—all seems well—turn my key in the door, and push. Inside, I'm met by the strong, disagreeable smell of cigar smoke. As soon as I close the door I can see up the hallway and into the living room. DS Mills is lounging on a sofa with his feet up on the coffee table. He is sucking on a cigar and holding a large goblet of brandy in his hand.

He looks at his cigar. 'You are late,' he says.

I glance at my watch. 'By a minute, Sir.'

'Arrive before I do, in future. I'm a busy man.' He gestures condescendingly with his finger to the sofa opposite him. 'Sit down.' Even beyond the office environment, his arrogance is breathtaking. I've heard that he is married, but I can't imagine the state of the long-suffering wife sitting at home waiting for him. I do as I am told.

'Spit it out then. What've you got for me on Eden?'

On the way here I'd thought of all the different ways I could tackle the subject with Mills, but face to face there is no easy way, so I just blurt it out.

'The information I have is not about Jake, Sir. It's about Robin.'

Mills' eyes narrow dangerously. He carefully places his cigar to rest on the side of his ashtray, and asks coldly, 'Is this some kind of bullshit joke, Strom?'

I stay strong. 'I'm afraid not, Sir. I have information that Robin has been seen in the Pilkingtons' clubs and I believe he might even be working with or for them.'

'You want me to believe this ludicrous accusation verbatim because?' His sarcasm and

irritation are obvious. He gets up onto his feet and walks around the sofa.

'I trust the source, Sir.'

'I'll be the judge of that. Who the fuck is your source?'

'A dancer from the club. She's seen Robin and Tommy Saunders, Billy Joe Pilkington's number two man, together at the club a few times. That is highly irregular and should be looked into.'

'A dancer?' he scoffs.

I swallow hard and sit upright. 'My duty is to put out any information I uncover so that any future investigations can be informed by it.'

'Robin can visit any damn club he wants. It's not against the law.'

I flush. 'My instinct tells me something more is going on, Sir. The dancer made some serious accusations. A girl he had gone out with went missing.'

'Do you think I'm going to take the word of some anonymous, two bit stripper over one of my best men? Have you and Eden cooked this cock and bull story up to save his ass?'

'That's not fair, Sir,' I snap back. 'I followed your instructions to the letter. No one, not even Jake Eden, knows about our arrangement.'

'I can't believe you dragged me up here for a bit of stripper gossip.'

'Have you got a magic crystal ball, Sir? Do you know exactly what is happening at all times and you never ever get anything wrong?'

He glares at me warningly. 'Watch yourself, Strom, I'm your commanding officer.'

But at this point I don't give a fuck anymore. He is just a bully. And I don't care if I never work in the force again. 'I'm just curious why you would not be even slightly intrigued as to why Robin might be fraternizing with well-known gangsters.'

'What are you implying, Strom?' Mills stops suddenly in my face. His face looks like it might explode among the bulging veins.

I remain outwardly calm and smile. 'I'm sure you can deduce the implication yourself, Sir.'

My sarcasm causes him to erupt violently. He thrusts a finger in my face. 'I'd be very careful, if I were you. You're walking on extremely thin ice.'

'I'm not afraid of you. I haven't done anything wrong. Yes, it was a lapse of judgment to sleep with my target, but I confessed, and offered to resign.'

Suddenly, like a bolt of lightning, out of nowhere, it comes to me. I see it clearly, the thing that had eluded me all this time, the thing that I had missed. I stare at him with shocked eyes. My eyes are riveted on him, equal parts fear and disbelief. My voice is a whisper. 'You showed no curiosity or surprise about the shipment coming in on the sixteenth. You knew about it before I told you, didn't you?'

He sighs. 'You stupid, stupid bitch. All you had to do was open your fucking legs and distract Eden while we laid our plans. But you couldn't just do that, could you? Oh no, you had to be a little Miss Marple, running around poking your fucking nose into things that have nothing to do with you.'

Suddenly I am afraid. I *have* been running around playing at being detective without any idea of what was really going on in the shadows. Jake is not the gangster. This man is. I see it in his cold, pitiless eyes.

The door. I have to get to the door. 'I'm not listening to this,' I say as calmly as I can manage, and getting up, head for the door. My knees are trembling so hard I am afraid I will not get to it. Almost there. I'm there... But before I can pull it open, Mills' big palm slams down on it.

I jump like a startled cat, a scream rattling in my throat.

'You're not dismissed yet,' he murmurs so close to my ear that I rear back in terror. He smiles at me and a shiver runs down my spine. There is something truly chilling and frightening about this smiling side of him. He is almost unrecognizable. I can hardly believe it is the same person. 'Back to your seat. I'm not quite finished with you.'

He is six feet plus and sixteen stone so my racing mind decides that it is best to placate him until I can think what to do next. I sit back down and watch him, frightened to my core.

He goes to the window, takes his mobile out of his belt holder and dials. While he waits for his call to be answered he keeps his eyes trained on me. I think about running to the door, but I know I won't make it. He is too fast. Too dangerous.

'Things have moved faster than expected,' he says into the phone. 'I'm going to need some help with dispatch.' A pause. 'No, no disposal necessary this time.' He listens again. 'Yes. Right now! Don't forget to knock three times, so I know it's you, and don't shoot you by mistake.' He laughs.

Oh my God! Oh my God. I am a dead woman... I have dug my own grave by doing such a good job of losing my tail. If Mills has his way, I will disappear without a trace. I think of Jake and everything he means to me.... God! He'll never know that I love him with all my heart. Oh God! I've been so, so stupid. What a mess I have made of everything.

Mills ends the call.

I need to think. I'm starting to feel out of control and hysterical. My mind tries to analyze the situation. Who has he called? Robin? Or maybe Tommy Saunders?

'Who have you just called?' I ask.

'That should be the least of your worries, I would have thought, Lily.'

Hearing him call me by my first name makes a wave of nausea roll into my stomach.

'You don't have to get rid of me. I'm off the force, anyway. Just let me go and you'll never hear from me again. I beg of you,' I cry. By his disgusted expression I know I sound whiny and pathetic, but I don't want to die. I want to live, I want to be with the man I love and watch our children playing in the meadows like Jake did on beautiful spring days.

'Don't be pathetic, Lily. We both know that's never going to happen. There's too much at stake for everyone concerned.'

Helpless and frightened tears run down my face. I start wailing.

'All right, I'll let you go.'

I stop and stare at him. He's playing games. 'You're going to let me go?' I know it is nonsense even as I say it.

'Yes, if you call Jake and ask him to come here now. It's not you I want.'

A strange kind of calm washes over me. There is not a single cell in me that can be persuaded to do that. I'll never hurt Jake. Not intentionally.

'I'd rather die than do that.'

Mills breaks into what can only be described as demonic laughter. All the hair on my arms stand. 'That's funny,' he says, getting a hold of himself. 'I'll just have to call him myself.'

'You don't have his number.'

'No, but you do.'

'I'll never give it to you.'

He starts walking toward me. I go rigid with fear. When he is about two feet away he reaches into his jacket, pulls out a gun and, after calmly screwing on the silencer, presses

the cold metal to my cheek. I emit an involuntary cry. 'Tell me,' he orders. My eyes swivel sideways and I stare at him in terror.

'Tell me or I'll blow your brains out.'

'No.'

He swings his hand in a wide arc and cracks the barrel of his gun across my temple. The blow sends me flying off my seat onto the floor, pain exploding in my head. I lie sprawled and stunned under the coffee table as he yanks my bag from my clenched fists. Through a haze of pain I see him search for my phone. I try to stand but he presses the heel of his shoe down on my chest and grins down at me.

Warm blood streams down my face. I start mumbling and begging him, 'No, please. Don't bring him here. Leave him alone.'

He walks away from me with the phone to his ear. I feel like I'm losing consciousness, but I know that I must stay awake no matter what. I must warn Jake, if it's the last thing I do. I hear him talking, but I can't make it out through the excruciating pain. Mills is coming back toward me.

He stands over me and calmly presses his heel into my hurt temple.

I scream.

'Is that proof enough for you or do I have to hurt her again?' he asks into the phone. I clench my teeth to stop myself from crying out and try to listen to Mills' side of the conversation. 'That's right. Get the key from under the mat and come in. Don't try anything funny or bring anyone else with you, or you'll be in time to see her skull explode.'

Mills ends the call and tosses my phone away. He then walks to the drinks cabinet and pours himself another brandy. He goes back to his chair and relights his cigar. He puts his gun in his lap and his feet up on the coffee table. He has assumed the same position I found him in. I hold my throbbing temple and remember my surveillance device. If I don't make it I need his confession on tape. Perhaps someone else will find it and put this corrupt bastard away.

'Why?' I ask. 'Why are you after Jake?'

He takes another mouthful of brandy. 'Why? Why anything, Strom? Territory... Money... Power... And a gangster I can control.'

'A gangster you can control?' I repeat.

He watches the smoke rising lazily from his cigar. 'You see, Lily, the real problem here is Eden. He's a fucking dinosaur and there's just no place for people like him in this industry.'

He takes a puff, blows out another plume of smoke and stares at me, his eyes dark and totally devoid of emotion. 'The people I work with can't have large swathes of prime real estate in the hands of someone like him. By running his clubs as if they're part of a legit business operation he's holding back progress.'

I make a small sound of disbelief. 'You mean Jake was telling me the truth! He really isn't a gangster?'

'Gangster?' Laughter erupts from his mouth. 'He's fucking soft in the head. With him out of the way the clubs will be run the way they should be. With the right working girls, and our own security people controlling the flow of drugs there's a fortune to be made.' He shrugs. 'I had a different timeline for our takeover, but with all your meddling and interfering you've pushed it forward. After today we'll have it all.'

'Just how do you plan to get away with this? You can't simply make Jake and me disappear. There'll be CCTV images of me and Jake coming here and questions that will eventually lead to you.'

Mills shakes his head. 'My dear naive Lily. It will be my team and me who will be investigating. It's really terribly simple and straightforward. Obviously, you discovered evidence of drug dealing. You came here to pass the information to me. Unknown to you your criminal husband followed you here. A gun battle ensued between him, my associate and me. Eden died. Unfortunately, Strom, you did too. Honorably in the line of duty. A real police hero. So young and good looking too – the papers will love it. We'll award you a medal for outstanding services or something. Your parents will be quite proud of you. The public will mourn the death of a brave officer. Obviously I take the credit for the bust, and Eden, a notorious criminal, is forgotten very quickly.'

I feel my stomach shrivel up inside my body as I hear his voice lay out the future so confidently. But when I speak my voice is full of contempt. At least I will die knowing that Jake is not criminal. He was being set up.

'I had you marked as the type of officer who retires on a nice pension in the countryside somewhere. But after today the only thing you will be looking forward to is a view of the inside of a cell for the remainder of your days.'

He laughs. 'It's kind of you to worry about my well-being when you're about to meet your maker.' He checks his watch.

'Is Robin coming?'

'You're giving me a headache, Strom. I'd appreciate a bit of quiet until your husband and my associate arrive.'

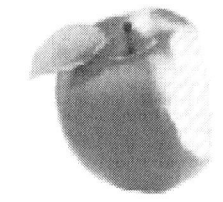

—You know it's true,
baby I'd die for you—

FOURTEEN

Jake

I feel the veins in my neck bulge, my throat narrow. If that fucking piece of dog shit harms one single hair on her head I'll kill him with my bare hands. My right leg starts trembling with nervous energy.

'God in heaven, why? Why, Lily? Why?' I smash my fist into the door. 'Why couldn't you just fucking leave me to deal with it?' Pain flowers into my fist. The pain is good, because it focuses my mind. I need to pull myself together. My secretary comes running into my office. Her eyes are wild. She has never seen me like this.

I hold my palms up.

'Do you want me to do anything?' she asks in a shocked tone.

I don't trust my voice. I shake my head and stride out through the open door. I drive back to the house in a state of such agitation that I speed through every single red light I come across. Horns blare at me from every direction. They increase my sense of panic. At an intersection I slam the steering wheel.

'Damn you, Lily. Always making promises you don't keep.'

I throw open the front door and race to my safe. There is an icy hand inside my chest: clenched around my heart. I'm so angry I could kill someone. I take out the gun, the one I had hoped I'd never have a need for again. I always knew taking this in my hands again would require a matter of life and death, and this is. I load it up, my movements precise and efficient. It's like riding a bike. You never forget. I slip it into my waistband. Then I slide the backup, a 9mm, into my right ankle holster and sprint to my car.

I input the address into my navigation system. Twenty-three minutes! That's how long it's going to take me to reach her. I tell myself to calm down, but I end up driving like a madman, keeping my foot floored to the pedal even when the near misses become more and more frequent. I sense that Lily's captor means business, but it is me he is after. She's just bait. And you don't hurt the hostage, at least, not until you get what you want.

In this case, me.

I pull up outside the address, adrenaline surging through my body. I switch off the engine and do a quick reconnaissance of the street. All seems quiet. I exit the car and walk quickly up to the discreet entrance. I press the buzzer as per instructions. Someone buzzes me in. Once inside the dimly lit foyer I see the two level staircase that leads up to the flat entrance at the top. I listen. Nothing. I take my gun out and climb the stairs. My heart is thumping so loud I can hear it in the echoing stillness of the stairwell.

I find a key under the mat and use it to push open the door. It swings back to reveal Lily sprawled on the ground and a large man is standing over her. A gun is pointed at her head and her face is chalk white and smeared with blood. I feel myself going into shock.

'Get out. Don't come in. He'll kill us both if you do,' she screams.

I came to get you and I'm not fucking leaving without you.

'Drop the gun, Eden, or I swear I'll splatter her brains right now.'

'Shoot her and you're dead.'

'But she'll be dead, too. You want to take that risk?'

I can see from the man's dead eyes that he is a psychopath. He wouldn't think twice about carrying out his threat. But I'm not giving up my gun, or both Lily and I are dead for sure. Two thoughts occur to me. He is alone. But he won't be so for long. This might be my only chance. My best hope is to distract the ugly cunt, and make him shoot at me, long enough for me to get a clear shot and finish him. I dive to the ground and roll, spin on the carpet, and bump into a lamp stand—it crashes to the ground. I lunge for the protection of a cabinet.

I see him: his eyes on fire, his shiny face contorted. He roars in surprise and rage, as he turns in my direction and starts firing wildly. The shots come rapidly. The shocking kick of the bullet as it smashes into my chest, shattering bone, muscles and sinew, whips me onto my back. The pain is ice-cold, fills my ravaged chest, and then something hits my head, it snaps back. Oh Jesus.... I pull myself upwards and level the arm that's still holding the gun. I pull the trigger.

He doesn't know what hit him as the bullet strikes him in the throat. His throat erupts. A spray of crimson paints the wall behind him as he sinks to the ground, clawing at his open throat, shrieking in agony. His body thrashes and writhes. Then an eerie silence descends. He is dead. I hear a sob, then an elongated wail of horror, the sound of cloth rustling. Lily is crawling toward me.

There is a strange icy throbbing in my chest, but my mind suddenly becomes calm and serene, almost trance-like. As if I am a calm observer. Outside the mayhem. At peace. Maybe I'm dying. Jesus, that would be a bummer. But at least it's done. The job's done. Lily is kneeling over me and crying, I feel a tear fall on my face. My head is on fire and I can feel my blood pouring out of me quickly. I try not to acknowledge it. I feel faint.

'It's all my fault. I'm sorry. I'm so sorry. I love you,' she sobs. 'I love you so much, Jake.'

Some part of me starts smiling. *Yeah, me too, babe. Like crazy.*

I try to speak, but my lungs are full of fluid, the agony is unspeakable. I try to squeeze her hand, but there appears to be no force in mine.

She starts shaking me. *Oh fuck's sake, Lily. Have a bit of respect. I'm dying here*, I want to joke, but my lips won't move. Oh Jesus, I cannot focus my eyes anymore. The peace envelops me like a fog. But I won't submit to it. I kick furiously against it.

'Don't you dare fucking die on me. Hold on, please, Jake.' She starts rummaging through the pockets of my jacket, finds my mobile, and dials. I don't want to die.

'Hurry, please,' she cries plaintively, urgently.

Suddenly I hear Lily drop the mobile phone without giving the address and scramble to her feet.

Oh my God! Something's wrong. She has my gun in her hand and is pointing it at someone standing in the doorway. I can't see who it is, I can't help her. Please... Get away, I want to scream. I try to rise up but I'm nailed to the floor.

I hear voices, Lily's and someone else's, a man's, but I'm drifting away...the blackness is calling.

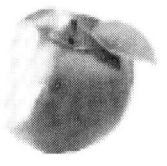

Lily

I hear him come up the stairs. My hands are shaking so much the gun seems to be rattling in my hands. I hate guns and I have only had two real hours of firearms training during the two week intensive. There is very little emphasis on SO10 operatives to master weapons since there is no need. Someone who can handle a gun will do so in the street compromising their cover. I take a deep breath. I curl my finger on the trigger. I straighten my elbows and point the gun into the open doorway. The sound of steps comes closer. I stare at the empty space.

Suddenly Billy Joe Pilkington fills the doorway. He is big. He is very big. And he has a gun.

'Don't come any further or I will shoot you,' I shout a warning.

FIFTEEN

Billy Joe Pilkington

'**W**hoa,' I say, dropping my gun and holding my exposed palms up. Hell, what the fuck happened here? I don't know what I expected, but not the one-man-down, Jake covered in blood on the ground, and his missus crazy-eyed and pointing a gun at me carnage I find.

'Hey, I'm here to help you.'

'Liar,' she screams wildly. 'I heard Mills call you and I know exactly what he said so don't try to pretend anything else. I'm not interested in your turf war. Just get out of here so I can call an ambulance and get Jake to hospital. If you don't leave I swear I'll shoot.'

'Listen, I'm not the snitch. Jake told me about it. It's Tommy. We figured it out.'

'So how did you know about this address? It's not listed anywhere,' she asks suspiciously, all the while glancing worriedly at Jake.

'We've been keeping a close eye on him. When he got a mobile call earlier today, he acted so nervous, I knew something was up. So I worked him over and that's when he told me about this place, you, and his bent fucking copper friend. I jumped in my vehicle and came straight here, tooled up and ready for fucking anything, but looks like I got here too late.'

Suddenly, she throws the gun to the floor. 'It's not you. You didn't knock three times.'

She doesn't make any sense but if she's putting down the gun, I'm made.

'I have to call an ambulance,' she blurts out, panicked and trembling.

I crouch over Jake. Fuck! He is in a bad way. He is lying in a pool of blood and more is pouring out of his head and chest. We can't wait for a fucking ambulance. He'll die before one gets here. The closest hospital is only ten minutes away. I might not even make it then.

I grab her wrist. Her eyes swing wildly toward me.

'Listen, we can't wait for an ambulance. We have to take him there ourselves. Do you understand me?'

She nods quickly.

'My car is double parked right outside. A blue—'

'I know it,' she cuts in impatiently.

'Right, I'm going to carry him. I want you to run ahead and open the back doors.'

I go to the curtain and tear a long strip. I tie it around his chest and around his head. Almost instantly the cloth becomes soaked. His breathing is scarily shallow. I don't waste any more time. I heave him off the ground. He's a big man, and unconscious he is a dead weight, but I have lifted men up and thrown them down from a high height during fights. I heave him up with a grunt and make for the stairs. Jake's wife has opened the car doors and has returned.

When she sees me she runs down the stairs ahead of me and holds open the door. I get him into the back of my car and while she cradles his head I run to the driver's seat and get in.

'Ready?'

'Go. Hurry, please,' she begs urgently.

I pull away and slam my foot on the accelerator. Some guy screams at me. 'Fucking maniac.' In ordinary circumstances I would have got out of the car, walked up to him and got him to say it to my face. He's got Jake to thank.

Jake's wife is crooning to him.

'Hang in there, Jake. I never said a bad thing about you. Not to anyone. Not ever. There was never anything bad to say. And I never gave a single important secret away. I'm good for all your secrets. I'll never talk. I'm your wife and I love you to bits. We have our whole lives to live. Don't leave me, my love. We will survive this. You just wait and see.'

The silence that comes from him is deafening.

I glance into the rear-view mirror and tears are pouring down her face. He lies in her lap with his eyes shut, so white, so still. It doesn't look good. This is the man who wouldn't lie

down and give up when he was in the ring with *me*. I feel the cold hand of real fear for him.

'Hang in there, Jake. Oh, Jake, Jake, Jake,' she sobs, while the blood seeps through her fingers. She looks up at me. She seems dazed and totally lost. I know her type. She's delicate. She can snap at any moment. I've seen that look before.

'His hair feels so soft and smells so good, but I can feel him slipping away. His pulse is slowing down, too. I think he's dying, BJ,' she tells me calmly.

Fuck me, if that isn't the weirdest thing I've heard today. She must be in shock and rambling. It's not going to be good when she zones back into reality.

I fucking nail my foot to the accelerator.

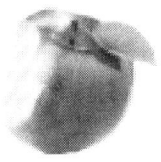

Lily

BJ gets Jake to the A & E of the closest hospital. I don't even register what it is called. I just sit there covered in his blood as they take him away from me and load him onto a gurney. It seems to me that they are moving too slowly.

I feel an irrational fury. I want to scream at them, but I don't. Instead they are surprised to find me perfectly calm. Even I am shocked at how unmoved I am. I don't feel *anything*.

'Hurry, please,' I urge, my voice, as cold as ice.

And they take him away from me.

Someone touches my arm. Slowly I swing my eyes upwards. A long way upwards. Ah, BJ.

'I've got to go. I can't be here when the police arrive.'

'OK. Thank you.'

'I'll be around later.'

He turns to move away. I catch his arm. 'Wait.'

He turns back, surprised.

I reach into my bra and fish out the surveillance stick. 'Can you hold onto this for me? You're the only one I can trust now.'

'What is this?'

'This is Jake's life.'

He takes it, nods, and leaves.

Then I call my old Detective Sergeant and give him the address, briefly warning him what his men are going to find. I take a deep breath and call Shane to ask him to come. As soon as I hear his voice that strange everything-is-under-control, all-is-well cloud that had protected me from fear and panic is suddenly gone.

My heart starts racing. My chest constricts and I can't catch my breath. Sweat starts pouring from my underarms. I feel lightheaded and faint. I am choked by a sensation that I could die right here from pure, unadulterated terror.

The terror of losing Jake.

Someone—a nurse—takes the phone from my rigid hand. Maybe she will tell Shane the name of the hospital. I become aware that other people in uniforms are running toward me. I see visions of me falling to the floor, screaming and kicking, and everyone staring curiously. My brain instructs me to tell the people who are holding me that it is Jake who needs their ministrations.

There seems to be confusion all around me.

Some rational part of my brain concedes that it is possible that I have become hysterical. In fact, I think I have just slapped a nurse. It's not that I want to, but I can't control my arms and legs. They flail out uncontrollably with a life of their own. Someone injects me with something.

I scream for my Jake until I am gone from my body.

SIXTEEN

Lily

I don't know how many hours pass before I wake up. There is no moment of confusion, of where am I? What is going on? Where is Jake? NO! As soon as I open my eyes I know. I am in a hospital and Jake's been taken away from me. He is probably being operated on. I sit up and slide off the bed. My bare feet touch cold ground. There are curtains pulled all around me. I part the curtains and start walking in the direction of voices. I come to the reception desk.

'Ah, you're awake,' someone says.

'Where's Jake?' I ask.

'Calm down.'

'I will calm down when you tell me where my husband is.'

'First we need some shoes,' she says.

'I just want to know—'

But she is already walking back to the curtained section where I had come from and returns with a pair of shoes, mine. I wear them hurriedly. 'Take me to my husband please.'

'He's still in surgery, but I can take you to where the rest of your family are.'

I frown. 'My family?'

'Yes, they are all waiting. Come on.'

I follow her to a sitting room. 'Here they are,' she says cheerfully.

The first person I see is Jake's mother.

The nurse makes her exit.

For a few seconds Jake's mother and I stare at each other. Then she stands up and advances toward me. Her small frame is trembling with anger. I look at her and I don't feel afraid. I want her to hurt me. I deserve it. It is all my fault. I was so stupid, so fucking careless. It will be a relief to have her strike me. She stands in front of me and lifts her hand. I think she intended to slap me. I would have done it if I were her. Her hand moves in an arc, but it never connects. Shane catches it.

'Don't, Ma,' he says sadly. 'He's in love with her. When he wakes up, it will break his heart to know you marked her.'

He lets go of her hand and she covers her mouth with it. Her eyes are shocked and huge and her hand is visibly shaking. 'What if he doesn't wake up?'

He turns white. 'Then his soul will grieve.'

She crumples then, sobbing as if her poor heart was breaking. He put his arm around her and gently led her toward the blue chair.

And then Dom is next to me. 'Come on,' he says. 'Let's get you some coffee.'

I let him lead me out of that sad waiting room with its blue seats and Jake's devastated mother.

I lean against the wall. Dom and I have hardly spoken. I've kept away from him.

'Do you want a real drink?' he says.

'Yeah,' I say.

He takes a flask out of his jacket pocket.

I take a long swallow. The alcohol burns my throat. 'How long has he been in the operating theater?'

'Seven hours.'

I become frightened. 'He's not going to make it, is he?'

His jaw goes stiff. 'He's gonna make it,' he says. 'He's gonna fucking make it or I'm gonna kill the fucking bastard myself.'

That's Dom for you: Why open a fucking door when you can fucking kick it down? Tears start flowing down my cheeks.

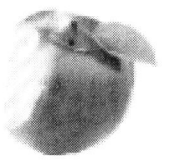

Jake

I wake up to indescribable pain. 'Lily,' I mutter.

There is no answer. I return to the blessed blackness.

I come back. Lights. Voices. Machines. Searing pain. I go away.

I open my eyes. A woman. 'Lily?'

'Nurse Bourne, I'm afraid.'

'Lily.'

'Your wife?'

'Yeah, my wife. Tell her to get her ass in here now,' I mumble.

And then it is blackness again.

My mother holds my hand. I know that. I feel her. She cries. I want to stop her. I'm all right. She goes. Shane comes. 'Get well soon,' he whispers.

I open my eyes and there she is. She is shaking. She puts her hand in mine. She's not all right. 'I love you,' she says. I'm not there for her.

Then I open my eyes and it is no longer fuzzy. I recognize my mother.

'Where's Lily, Ma?' I ask.

'She's outside,' she says. 'You nearly died because of her.'

'That's right. I nearly died because of her, but I'd be dead without her, Ma. She warned us they had infiltrated BJ's organization.'

That's the thing about Ma, she's not vindictive. She forgives easily. 'In that case I will pray to the Madonna for your wife,' she whispers.

A little while after, Ma leaves and Lily opens the door.

'Oh, you're awake,' she cries with disbelief.

She comes and stands beside me, fragile as a bit of porcelain. There is a bandage on her temple and a long bruise on her left cheek and blue shadows under her eyes, but she is still so beautiful I want to weep.

'I can't wait to get my cock into your pussy,' I tell her and she begins to cry. Huge big tears that roll down her cheeks. I don't stop her. I know they are tears of joy.

SEVENTEEN

Lily

If I had not made the recording I don't know how it would have turned out. For many days the papers ran with the story and it was big news. We killed a DS, a highly respected one at that. I told them everything I knew, but I don't know what happened to Robin. Once I called the office and asked for him. One of the guys picked up the phone and told me he doesn't work there anymore. I never saw anything in the papers so I guess they just did what they always do. Cover their own asses.

It is nearly two weeks before we are allowed to take Jake home. The family rallies round. Shane and Dom set up a bed downstairs in one of the reception rooms so Jake doesn't have to go up the stairs to sleep. Shane and Dom carefully lay him in bed. I hover around helplessly behind them. Jake has become so pale.

'Thanks,' he tells his brothers.

I offer them a drink but they leave pretty quickly once Jake has been installed.

'Back later tonight,' they tell me.

'OK,' I say as I close the front door. I go back to the living room and Jake is grinning at me.

'God, I've missed being home with you,' he says. 'Come and kiss me properly then,' he says.

I go over feeling suddenly shy. I've told him that I love him, but I don't know whether he heard. If he can still remember what happened after his head trauma.

I kiss him gently on the lips and his hand comes around my forearm. 'You call that measly thing a kiss?'

I laugh. 'You're supposed to take it easy.'

'I'm supposed to, but you're not.'

I frown at him. 'What are you talking about?'

'Take off your panties.'

'What?'

'You heard.'

'Why?'

'Don't make me get up and bust all these stitches.'

'This is crazy. I can't believe you're doing this,' I say, taking my panties off. 'Right. They're off. Happy now?'

'Come closer,' he invites, his eyes alive with something I haven't seen for two weeks. Something I was afraid I would never see again.

'Listen, you're not allowed—'

'To strain. I'm not going to strain. You are.'

I bite my lip. I want to go over, but I really don't want to do anything that could harm him.

'If you don't come, I'm coming to get you,' he warns.

I look at him worriedly. 'Jake...'

'I promise I'm not going to move a muscle. You're going to do all the work.'

I take the step closer.

'Spread your legs.' His voice holds an implacable quality.

I inch my legs apart, feeling myself getting wetter.

'Open for me, Lily,' he persuades.

I spread my legs farther apart and he slips his hand between my legs, slipping his fingers into the crack, playing with the wet folds, collecting my arousal on his fingers. Taking it to his mouth. And sucking it off.

'Take your top and your bra off.'

I obey.

'And your skirt.'

He buries his fingers in me. Totally naked with his fingers working on me I moan. 'Lift one leg and put it on the mattress.' With my hands resting on the mattress I lift one leg and rest it on the bed as he commands That opens me up to his gaze. I look down myself at the end of his hand. Dirty. Dirty. Dirty.

My nipples start aching. I am mad for the feel of his mouth on them, sucking, licking, biting. Watching me avidly he glides one finger into me. I shudder, my back arching. He slips his finger out and circles my clit. I push my hips desperately against his hand, wanting the finger back, the blood running hot in my veins.

Two fingers enter me. I whimper. His touch slows. The fingers withdraw. A small cry of frustration erupts from my mouth. His fingers hover over the entrance of my sex. I push my hips forward chasing those elusive fingers. He lets me catch his fingers. They slide in.

He stops moving. I look at him, my body twisted, begging for more.

'If you want it, work for it,' he says. 'Fuck my fingers.'

So I do. I ram into his fingers, two then three, stretching me. My hands are numb from gripping the mattress so hard and my body being twisted uncomfortably. Every thrust increases the discomfort but that is part of the pleasure, too. The pleasure of being overwhelmed, commanded and watched while I fuck his fingers with what should have been shame but isn't. He watches me avidly until the climax comes for me.

'Oh God!' I scream, feeling myself fly again with the sensation of being unspeakably filthy, of being wanted so violently by this man. It has been so long.

Naked and strangely exhausted I climb into bed and carefully lie beside him. For a while neither of us speaks.

'Jake.' I lift myself onto my elbow. 'Do you remember what happened in that flat?'

'Some,' he says, turning his head to look at me.

'Do you remember what I told you?'

His eyes gleam. 'Tell me again what you told me and I will see if I remember it,' he says innocently.

I smile. 'I meant every word,' I say.

'Is it beautiful yet?'

I frown. 'Is what beautiful?'

'Remember when you said love should be beautiful. Is it beautiful yet?'

My eyes fill with tears. 'Yes, it's beautiful.'

'I'm glad,' he says softly. 'Because it was always beautiful for me. Our meeting was a "magic" of perfect timing. A few seconds later and you would have gone through that side door and we would never have met. I knew from the moment our eyes met that you were mine. And you were already mine in many other lifetimes.' He reaches his hand out to touch my face, the skin softened by days of lying in bed. 'I've always loved and I'll always love you. No matter what they throw at us they will never separate us. Even our separation will be illusions. After this life is over I will seek you again, and I will find you again.'

It dawns on me as I look into Jake's eyes, that losing Luke tore the life from me, but then the same random hand that took him away intervened again and made the most unlikely suitor become my savior. A tear crawls down my cheek. Maybe I always knew from our first kiss that he was the only one who could have mended my heart.

He smiles gently, my beautiful, beautiful gangster man.

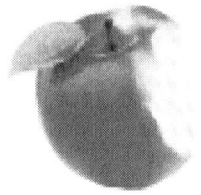

—Baby, it's only for you, it's only for you
Baby, it's only for you, only for you—

EPILOGUE

Lily

I have named them all. That huge one over there is Jakob; his wife is called Elsie. No, I'm not being facetious, she *is* his wife, once mated, male and female crows stay together for life. I have seen their chicks: beautiful, with bits of yellow on their bills and blue-eyed. I call to Elsie and she flies over and lands on my shoulder. I turn my head and she rubs her beak against my nose. I know most people think that crows are a dull black, but in fact, they have a light violet gloss on their bodies and a greenish-blue gloss on their wings. The violet gloss gleams in the sunlight. I know why Jakob chose her. She is beautiful.

When Elsie flies back to her mate I walk away. Soon I will have a chick of my own. Two months ago I stopped taking the pill and this morning I peed on a stick that came up with a thin blue line. For a few seconds I had stared at the stick in shock. Unable to move, something irrepressible opening up like a flower inside me.

I wanted to run into the bedroom and tell Jake straightaway, but I decided to save the news. After dinner tonight. He is taking me away to Paris. I will tell him then. Mine was in a bathroom but let him remember the moment as something truly special.

A gift on the anniversary of our meeting.

A small smile comes to me at the thought of his expression. I know he wants a big family. He has even got names all planned for them. He says he wants at least half a dozen, but obviously he's not getting that. He tried to pin me down to five. I said two. He said four and we finally agreed on three. But in fact, I am open to four. It all depends on how painful childbirth turns out to be.

I hope my baby will be green-eyed like him.

The coming of the child makes my thoughts turn to Luke. I don't dream so much of him anymore. At first I was sad. As horrible as they were, I felt with their passing, I had lost my last connection to him, but then I realised that the nightmares are not my connection to him. The memory of him doing handstands in the rain, building a snow staircase to Santa Claus and the hundreds of other memories of him are what's left of him.

The sky is blue and the sun is warm on my back. I shade my eyes and look to the distance. I can see Jake riding Thor. He is coming in my direction. As ever he is not wearing a shirt. The wind whips at his hair. I feel the vibration of the horse and the man even before I hear them.

My heart swells with love. I smile up at him. The horse snorts and looks at me with big, liquid eyes. From my pocket I take out a lump of sugar and hold it in the palm of my hand. The horse goes for it. His rough lips brush my skin. Jake gets off, picks me up by the waist and whirls me around.

'Hey,' I say, laughing. 'What's this in aid of?'

'Nothing. Every time I see you I feel such a rush of joy it has to be acted on.'

I put my hands on either side of his cheeks, look into those gorgeous, magnificent, grass-green eyes of his, and bending my head, kiss him. 'I love you, Jake Eden. So damn much.'

And it's true. I'm crazy about him. He has totally changed my life. I was covered in cobwebs in a cold, dark place until he laid eyes on me. He never took no for answer. And never gave up on me. Ever. He hung in there no matter how bad it looked. He is truly as he says. As tenacious as a gnarled tree.

'I hope you never tire of telling me that,' he says, gently setting me down on the ground.

'Want some breakfast?' I ask.

'What am I having?'

'What do you want?'

'Well, today is our anniversary so I want something special.'

I look up at him. His skin is tanned and healthy and there is a cheeky smile playing about his mouth. One day his skin will crinkle and hang off his bones, but even then I will never tire of looking at him.

'Well, come into the kitchen then,' I say.

He fakes wretchedness. 'There was a time you would have called me into the bedroom.'

I laugh and open the kitchen door. 'Did you or did you not have an anniversary blowjob *and* an anniversary fuck this morning, Jake Eden?'

'I'll admit, I did.'

I step inside. It is cool in the house. I go to one of the cabinets and open it. 'So...'

He grins. 'I was hoping for something a bit more on our anniversary.'

When he is like this I find him impossible to resist. I take out a wooden box and open it.

Jake comes close. 'Did they bring you something else today?'

I take a bit of a child's broken plastic toy out of my pocket. Red and blue. I hold it out to him.

He takes it out of my palm and examines it. 'Fucking hell, it's hard to keep up with these critters. They keep bringing stuff for my wife.'

I suppress the laughter that is rising in my throat. 'I have an Irish joke for you.'

He groans. 'Not another one?'

God! How much I love, love, love this man. 'Do you want to hear it or not?'

'Does it feature a fork and soup rain?'

'No.'

He leans his hip against the edge of the counter. 'All right then.'

'The thing is, this joke can only be told in the bedroom.'

'Lead the way, madam,' he says, straightening himself eagerly, his eyes shining.

Well, the joke had eight canned pineapple rings and a bit of whipped cream, but my husband is big, so I had to use twelve pineapple rings and half a can of whipped cream.

Did my husband enjoy the joke?

Yeah, any hot-blooded Irishman would. It was good enough to eat.

And guess who ate it?

Yeah, me. I'd eat anything off that Irishman...

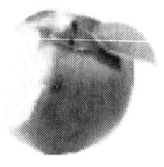

In memory of Patrick Eden:

Muldoon lived alone in the Irish countryside with only a pet dog for company. One day the dog died, and Muldoon went to the parish priest and said, 'Father, my dog is dead. Could ya be sayin' a mass for the poor creature?'

Father O'Malley replied, 'I'm afraid not; we cannot have services for an animal in the church. But there are some Baptists down the lane, and there's no tellin' what they believe. Maybe they'll do something for the creature.'

Muldoon said, 'I'll go right away, Father. Do ya think five thousand is enough to donate to them for the service?'

Father O'Malley exclaimed, 'Sweet Mary, Mother of Jesus! Why didn't ya tell me the dog was Catholic?'

Hello ☺,

If you have enjoyed EDEN you might like a peek into what happens to BJ and Layla. Their sweltering affair is called **Sexy Beast** and will be available in the summer of 2015.

Click on the link below to receive news of my latest releases, great giveaways, and exclusive content.
http://bit.ly/1oe9WdE

On another note...

Want To Leave A Review?

No matter how short it may be, it is *precious*. Please use these links:

United States
http://www.amazon.com/dp/B00SXETD8U/

United Kingdom
http://www.amazon.co.uk/gp/product/B00S XETD8U

Canada
http://www.amazon.ca/gp/product/B00SXE TD8U

Australia

http://www.amazon.com.au/gp/product/B00SXETD8U

I **LOVE** hearing from readers so do come and say hello here:
https://www.facebook.com/georgia.lecarre

xx Georgia

Coming Next...

Unlocking her mind...
Will unleash his darkest desires.

Hypnotized

#1 *AMAZON* BESTSELLING AUTHOR
GEORGIA LE CARRE

Hypnotized

Georgia Le Carre

The power of a glance has been so much
abused in love stories, that it has come to be
disbelieved in. Few people dare now to say that
two beings have fallen in love because they
have looked at each other. Yet it is in this way
that love begins, and in this way only.

—Victor Hugo, *Les Misérables*

Prologue

The girl behind the counter smiled at me and licked her lips. Shit. That was an invitation if ever I saw one. Sorry, honey, I'm married. Hey, I'm not just married, I'm in fucking love. I had the perfect life. A beautiful wife, two little terrors, a successful career. In fact, I was poised to dominate my industry.

The results of my research would soon be made public and I was going to be a star! Life was good.

'Keep the change,' I told her.

Her smile broadened and yet there was disappointment in her eyes.

I grinned and shrugged. 'If I wasn't already hooked I'd ask you out. You're gorgeous.'

'I'm not jealous,' she said flirtatiously.

'My wife is,' I told her, and picked up the tray of drinks: cappuccino for me, latte for my wife, and two hot chocolates for my monsters. Suddenly I heard a man shout, 'Fuck me!' And though those two words had nothing to do with me, my body— No, not just my body, *every part* of me *knew*.

They concerned me.

I whirled around, jaw clenched, still clutching the paper tray of drinks—one cappuccino, one latte, and two hot chocolates— as if it was my last link to normality. For

precious seconds I was so stunned, I froze. I could not believe what I was seeing. Then instinct older than life kicked in. The tray dropped from my hand—one cappuccino, one latte, and two hot chocolates—my last link with normality falling away from me forever. I began to race toward the burning car. My car. With my family trapped in it. I could see my babies screaming and banging on the car doors.

'Get out, get out of the fucking car,' I screamed as I ran.

I could see them pulling at the handles, their small spread palms banging desperately on the glass. I could even see their little mouths screaming for me.

'Daddy, Daddy.'

It was shocking how frightened and white their little faces were. I could not see my wife. Where was she?

I was running so fast my legs felt as if they might buckle, but it was as if I was in slow motion. Time had slowed down. At that moment thoughts came into my head at sonic speed, but the disaster carried on in real time. Suddenly my wife lifted her head and I saw her. She was looking out through the window directly at me. I was twenty feet away when I saw everything clearly. I kept on running, but it was like being in a dream where your mother suddenly turns into an elephant.

You don't go *What the fuck?*

You just carry on as normal even though your mother has just turned into a green elephant. I just carried on running. I no longer looked at my children. My gaze was riveted by the sight of my wife. I was ten feet away when the car exploded. Boom! The force of it picked me up and threw me backwards. I flew in the air and landed hard on the tarmac. I did not feel the pain of the impact. I got onto my elbows and watched the fire consume my family and the thick, black smoke that poured from the wreckage.

There was no grief then. Not even horror. It was just shock. And the inability to comprehend. The loss, the carnage, the tragedy, the green elephant. People came to help me up. I was shaking uncontrollably. They thought I was cold so they wrapped me in blankets. They sent me in an ambulance to the hospital. I never spoke. The whole time I was trying to figure out the green elephant. Why? How? It confused me. It destroyed my life, past, present and future.

Two years later
London

Marlow Kane

It is the time you have wasted for your rose that
makes your rose so important.
—Antoine de Saint-Exupéry, *The Little Prince*

'**L**ady Swanson is here for her appointment,'
Beryl said into the intercom. Even her voice
was all at once professional and terribly
impressed.

'Send her in,' I said and rose from my desk.

The door opened and a classically beautiful
woman entered. Her skin was very pale and as
flawless as porcelain. It contrasted greatly with
her shoulder-length dark hair and intensely
blue eyes. Her dress and long coat were in the
same cream material; her shoes exactly
matched the color of her skin. The overriding

impression was of an impossibly wealthy and elegant woman. Women like her lived in movies and magazines. They did not walk into the consulting rooms of disgraced hypnotists.

'Lady Swanson,' I said.

'Dr. Kane,' she murmured.

I winced inwardly. 'Just Marlow, please,' I said and gestured toward the chair.

She came forward and sat. She crossed her legs. They were long and encased in the sheerest tights I had seen in my life. Yes, she was an incredibly polished and cultivated woman.

I smiled.

She smiled back nervously.

'So, I believe you refused to tell Beryl your reason for coming to see me?'

'That is correct.'

'What can I do for you, Lady Swanson?'

'It's not for me. It's for my daughter. Well, she's my stepdaughter, but she is just like my own. I've raised her since she was two years old. She's twenty now.'

I nodded and began to raise the estimation of her age upwards. She must have been at least forty, but she didn't look a day over twenty-eight.

'Her name is Olivia and she met with an accident about a year ago.' Lady Swanson paused for breath. 'She nearly died. She had extensive injuries and was in hospital for many months. When she recovered she had lost her memory. She can remember nothing. She can remember how to do *things*—cook, places—but she cannot remember her past.'

I nodded.

'I was hoping hypnotherapy could help her remember her past.' She leaned forward slightly, her lips parted. 'Do you think you could...hypnotize her?'

I watched her and thought of the men in her life. How easy it must have been for such a beautiful woman to get anything she wanted from a man.

'Lady Swanson, I'm not sure I am the right man for the job. Usually I treat people who want to lose weight, kick a bad habit, or who are afraid of spiders.'

'I understand that, but do you think you could help her, though?'

'To be honest, I've never had such a patient.'

'Well, it's worth a try then?' she pressed hopefully.

'But you have to bear in mind that not everybody can be hypnotized.'

She didn't listen to that. Instead she broke into a smile. It was like the sun shining out from between a crack in a sky full of storm clouds. Yes, she was obviously one of those women who could whistle a chap off a tree, but... I was immune to it. For two years I had wandered around looking for even the smallest spark of the vibrant life that used to course through my veins. All I had ever found was ashes. Even now this beautiful, beautiful woman elicited nothing from me.

'Oh that's wonderful,' she gushed softly. 'You will take her on then?'

I felt almost as if she had subtly manipulated me. 'I'll try. No promises.'

'I did some research on you and your work, and I am certain you are the best person for the job. If anybody can do it, you can.'

I froze at that.

Instantly her face lost some of its glowing enthusiasm. 'I hope you don't think I was snooping into your private affairs? I was only interested in your professional credentials...'

I smiled tightly: the personal stuff came up with the professional stuff. After the accident the two had become inextricably entwined. 'Of course not. It is prudent to check out a practitioner before you go to see him.'

'I just want what is best for my daughter. And you are that. Will you take on her case?'

'Does your stepdaughter know you are here?'

She leaned back and looked out of the window. 'A butterfly wing is a miracle, made up of thousands of tiny, loosely attached pigmented scales that individually catch the light and together create a depth of color and iridescence unmatched elsewhere in nature. Our identities are like the butterfly wing, made up of thousands and thousands of tiny, loosely attached memories. Without them we lose our color and iridescence. Olivia is like a child now. We make all the major decisions for her. The world is a frightening place for her.'

'All right, Beryl will find an appointment for you.'

She smiled. A soft smile. And I had a vision. Her in bed with her shriveled husband. It was not only she who had done a quick Google search. It was not every day that Lady Swanson, of the Swanson dynasty, called my office for an appointment.

For a moment our eyes held and I saw something in hers. Interest. Desire. I let my eyes slide away.

'Thank you... Marlow.'

'Goodbye, Lady Swanson.'

'Ivana, please.'

'Goodbye, Ivana.'

I walked to the door, opened it, and let her out. As she passed me her perfume wafted into my nostrils. Expensive, faint, but still heady. From up close she was even more flawless. I closed the door and walked to my desk. I opened my drawer and taking out a bottle of Jack Daniel's poured myself a huge measure. I knocked it back, swallowed, and closed my eyes. Fuck. Was it ever going to stop hurting? I walked to the window and watched Lady Swanson get into her chauffeur-driven Rolls-Royce Phantom. She stared straight ahead. It was almost as if it was only a dream that she had come into my office and sat in my chair.

The intercom buzzed. 'Can I come in?' Beryl asked.

I sighed. 'Yes.'

The door opened even before I had taken my finger away from the button.

'Well?' she asked, wide-eyed. 'That was a very short first session. What did she want?'

'She wants me to treat her stepdaughter.'

Her eyes became huge. 'What? She wants you to treat Lady Olivia?'

'How did you know that?'

'It was all over the papers. She met with an accident and lost her memory. You have your work cut out for you.'

'Why do you say that?'

'Lady Olivia is known in the tabloids as 'Miss Secretive'. She has never ever given an interview and furiously guards her privacy. There are no pictures of her behaving badly. Ever.' Beryl came deeper into the room and went to my computer. She typed in a few words and turned towards me, her face filled with gossipy excitement, said, 'Here. This is what she looks like.'

I walked toward the computer screen.

It was not a very good picture. A long lens photo. Grainy. And not even in color. But my cock twitched and woke up from its deep sleep.

Coming Soon...

GOLD DIGGER

Georgia Le Carre

CHAPTER 1

'**W**hatever you do, don't *ever* trust them. Not one of them,' he whispered. His voice was so feeble I had to strain to catch it.

'I won't,' I said, softly.

'They are dangerous in a way you will never understand. Never let your guard down,' he insisted.

'I understand,' I said, but all I wanted was for him to stop talking about them. These last precious minutes I didn't want to waste on them.

He shook his head unhappily. 'No, no, you don't understand. You can never let your guard down for even an instant. Never.'

'All right, I won't.'

'I will be a very sad spirit if you do.'

'I won't,' I promised vehemently, and reached for his hand. The contrast between my hand and his couldn't have been greater. Mine was smooth and soft and his was gnarled and full of green veins, the skin waxy and liver-spotted. The nails were the color of polished ivory. The hand of a seventy-year-old man. His fingers grasped fiercely at my hand. I lifted them to my lips and kissed them one by one, tenderly.

His eyes glowed briefly in his wasted, sunken face. 'How I love you, my darling Tawny,' he murmured.

'I love you. I love you. I love you,' I said.

'Do your part and they cannot touch you.'

He sighed. 'It's nearly time.'

'Don't say that,' I cried, even though I knew in my heart that he was right.

His eyes swung to the window. 'Ah,' he sighed softly. 'You've come.'

My gaze chased his. The window he was looking at was closed, the heavy drapes pulled shut. Goose pimples crawled up my arms. 'Don't go yet. Please,' I begged.

He dragged his gaze reluctantly from the window. His thin, pale lips rose at the edges as he drew in a rattling breath. 'I've got to go, my darling. I've got to pay my dues. I haven't been a good man.'

'Just wait a while.'

'You have your whole life ahead of you.'

He turned his unnaturally bright eyes away from me, looked straight ahead, and with a violent shudder, departed.

For a few seconds I simply stared at him. Appropriately, outside the October wind howled and dashed itself into the shutters. I knew the servants were waiting downstairs. Everyone was waiting for me to go down and tell them the news. Then I leaned forward and put my cheek on his still, bony chest. He smelled strongly of medicine. I closed my eyes tightly. Why did you have to go and die and leave me to the wolves?

In that moment I felt so close to him I wished that this time would not end. I wished I could lie on his chest, safe and closeted away from the cruel world. I heard the clock ticking. The flames in the fireplace crackled and spat. Somewhere a pipe creaked. I placed my chin on his chest and turned to look at him one last time. He appeared to be sleeping. Peaceful at any rate. I stroked the thin strands of white hair lying across his pinkish white scalp, and let my finger run down his prominent nose. It shocked me how quickly the tip of his nose had lost warmth. Soon all of him would be stone cold.

I wondered whom he had seen at the window. Who had come to take him to his reckoning. My sorrow was complete. I could put my fingertips into it and feel the edges. Smooth. Without corners. Without sharpness. It had no tears. I knew he was dying two hours before. Strange because it had seemed as if he had taken a turn for the better. He seemed stronger, his cheeks pink, his eyes brilliantly bright and when he smiled it appeared as if he was lit from within. He even looked so much stronger. I asked him what he wanted to eat.

'Milk. I'll have a glass of milk,' he said decisively.

But after I called for milk and it was brought to him he smiled and refused it. 'Isn't this wonderful?' he asked. 'I feel so good.'

And at that moment I knew. Even so it was incomprehensible to me that he was really gone. I never wanted to believe it.

'In the end you wanted to go, didn't you?'

There was no answer.

'It's OK. I know you were tired. It was only me holding you back. You go on ahead. Find a place for me.'

He lay as still as a corpse. Oh God! I already missed him so much.

'I understand you can't talk. But you can hear me. When it is my turn I want you to come and get me. I'll be expecting you to come in through the window. Go in peace now, my love. All will be well. They will never know the truth. I will never tell them. To the day you come back to collect me.'

And then I began to cry, not loud, ugly sobs, but a quiet weeping. I didn't want the servants to hear. To come rushing in. Call the doctor waiting downstairs to come in and pronounce him dead. I knew what waited for me outside this room. Another hour...or two wouldn't make a difference. This was my time. My final hours with my husband.

The time before I became the hated gold digger.

17400439R00111

Printed in Great Britain
by Amazon